DEMON'S
BLUFF

RENEGADE SPIRIT SERIES

Tattooed Rats
Demon's Bluff

DEMON'S BLUFF

A NOVEL

RENEGADE SPIRIT: BOOK TWO

JERRY B. JENKINS
& JOHN PERRODIN

THOMAS NELSON
Since 1798

NASHVILLE   DALLAS   MEXICO CITY   RIO DE JANEIRO   BEIJING

Published in Nashville, Tennessee. Thomas Nelson is a trademark of Thomas Nelson, Inc.

Thomas Nelson, Inc. titles may be purchased in bulk for educational, business, fund-raising, or sales promotional use. For information, please e-mail SpecialMarkets@ThomasNelson.com.

Scripture quotations are taken from the New King James Version. Copyright © 1982 by Thomas Nelson, Inc. Used by permission. All rights reserved.

Publisher's Note: This novel is a work of fiction. Names, characters, places, and incidents are either products of the author's imagination or used fictitiously. All characters are fictional, and any similarity to people living or dead is purely coincidental.

Library of Congress Cataloging-in-Publication Data

Jenkins, Jerry B.
   Demon's Bluff / Jerry B. Jenkins and John Perrodin.
     p. cm. — (Renegade spirit ; bk. 2)
   Summary: At the insistence of the Tattooed Rats, Patch Johnson is hiding out in Demon's Bluff, Nevada, a town known for its annual Spirit Fest, and many of his friends and enemies are drawn there as the next battle between angels and demons looms.
   ISBN-13: 978-1-59145-397-0 (hardcover)
   ISBN-10: 1-59145-397-6 (hardcover)
   [1. Faith—Fiction. 2. Good and evil—Fiction. 3. Christian life—Fiction. 4. Angels—Ficiton. 5. Demonology—Fiction. 6. Nevada—Fiction.] I. Perrodin, John. II. Title.
PZ7.J4138Dem 2007
[Fic]—dc22

Printed in the United States of America
07 08 09 10 QW 6 5 4 3 2

To Sue. God's answer to my prayers.
—John Perrodin

With the rise of the World Peace Alliance, teens who claim the name of Christ are treated as lepers; their citizenship is denied, and their families are torn apart. As a member of the Tattooed Rats, Patch Johnson has discovered that living for himself brings only heartache. Slowly, painfully, he has learned to accept the high price of loving his enemies. He's also found faithful new friends, fought raging demons, and discovered that hope lives—even in the darkest places.

The Kids

Patrick "Patch" Johnson: A teen who's been given a new chance in a new town and wants only to fit in. After being torn away from his friends, he must ask himself what God desires.

Erin: She calls herself a Christian but wonders what that really means.

Molly: An outspoken teen who's not afraid to ask tough questions.

Granger: A basketball player who questions if there's more to life than food, fun, and girls.

Claudia: "The Claw" controls others by using secrets as weapons.

Trevor: Claudia's handsome friend, a demon who is willing to do anything to hurt Patch. He's training Hope and Barry, two demons he's forced to mentor.

Nancy: The do-gooder, volunteer, bookworm. All she cares about is making good grades and not being singled out for attention.

Jarrod: A disabled teen who gets around more quickly on crutches than most do on two good feet. His greatest hope is to have Jesus heal him.

The Adults

Cheryl McCry: Devoted to the destruction of Christians and a leader in the World Peace Alliance, the one-world regulatory system. She must capture Patch or her reputation will be destroyed.

Pastor Ron: Jarrod's minister, a prayer warrior.

1

CLAUDIA CURLED UP in the window seat, her fat cat snoring in her lap. But she wasn't thinking about the animal as she stroked its thick white fur. Not for a second. Tall, handsome Trevor captured her mind, then smeared it with memories of the night she'd found him in a heap on the street.

Maybe she'd only imagined Trevor had shed his skin like a snake, leaving it in a pile. He was like a nice guy. Really nice—probably just another ordinary teenager like her.

Yeah, right. She'd seen what she'd seen.

Claudia puffed out her cheeks, overcome with worry. She had to face facts. Trevor was a demon . . . and yet, still her friend. That was okay even if it was weird.

"Right, Lucy?"

The cat snubbed her, squeezing its pudgy eyes tight as Claudia continued to pet it with her painted nails.

Why did Trevor pretend to be a high school student when he was a freak? What was the point? Claudia pressed her temples. This didn't make sense. She'd sure never look at a handsome guy the same way. A couple of years of high school and she had already learned that.

She'd also learned no one dared to discuss the night Trevor had disappeared and Patch was hauled away, which frustrated Claudia. She wanted to talk it out, to understand.

She laid the sleepy cat onto the floor, padded barefoot into the kitchen, and stacked half a dozen fudge cookies next to the fruit on her plate. In the summer she could do what she wanted: watch movies, eat, shop, eat, nap like her cat. Then have another snack.

Claudia had almost three whole months of freedom before her. She could be gone all day and no one would miss her.

P ATCH WAS THIRSTY. "Any more juice?"

Snips, the tattooed barber from New Peace Clinic, popped open the cooler between the front seats of the van. "Grape okay?" He also tossed Patch a package of sealed crackers with pale orange spread mushed between them.

Patch didn't know how to act, what to say. One moment he'd been turned over to Cheryl McCry, the wickedest witch in the World Peace Alliance. The next he was heading north with a couple of Tattooed Rats—friends willing to risk their lives for his safety.

He glugged down the rest of his juice. "Can't you at least tell me where we're going?"

"Don't know yet." It was the woman, the orderly who had helped Patch at the clinic a few weeks before. She'd stopped giving Patch sedatives and substituted sugar pills—anything to jump-start his foggy brain. She was a quiet person; they had ridden several hundred miles before she'd said a word the night they rescued him: "I'm Laura. And I'm really shy."

So brave and yet still afraid.

Now she added, "We really don't know where we're going to end up. We've got a spot on the map to try to reach each night."

Snips wore short sleeves that revealed muscled arms and shiny black tattoos of scenes from the Bible. "We get the next spot each time we arrive."

"Kind of spiritual, huh?" Patch said.

"Oh, no, he's going deep on us again," Snips said, but Laura had reclined her seat and shut her eyes.

"We don't know what God has for us from one day to the next," Patch said.

Laura popped her seat back up. "Never thought of it that way." She had dark black curls, and something about her chin reminded Patch of his late mom. How he missed his parents and his little sister.

2

T HE COURSE WAS called "Teen Manipulation: Dos and Don'ts." Trevor had a goal. He wanted to learn how to effectively destroy the teenaged targets he'd been assigned to attack. This was his life's work. Torment was his pleasure. That's why he always listened carefully in class.

His dragon-shaped head tipped down, boxy eyes wide. He bit his scaly lip as his spiked tail twitched.

"You disgusting, selfish worm." The teacher, Flabbygums, a hunched demon, leaned into Trevor's face. "All you thought about was your own survival."

The rest of the class, made up of demons with varying levels of experience in harassing adolescent humans, nudged each other, delighted in seeing the smug devil disciplined. Their murmurs morphed into growls, then roars. Trevor wanted to cover his ears and run. But he stood, big feet planted. He almost wished he was wearing his "cool teen guy" outfit and not singled out for the spotlight.

"Excellent work," Flabbygums said, smiling, fangs dripping. "Extra credit for escaping."

Trevor let his teeth show, throwing his head back and shrieking with laughter. He was right and they were wrong. All of them. Again.

He listened to the mumbles, the curses. They hated him and he knew why. He was the best at what he did. Everyone wished they had his talent.

"Watch and learn," Trevor hissed as he returned to his desk and his classmates silently pulled claws, hooves, and tails out of his path. "Move or I'll stomp you."

The ancient instructor, who'd escaped the withering heat of the abyss for centuries, pulled down the screen. "Let's watch that attack again and see if we can figure out what went wrong. And why Trevor's timely retreat made so much sense."

Trevor crossed his arms, chewed the jagged tip of one claw, and pointed with his tail. "The good part's coming up."

So IT NEVER happened. None of it." Claudia curled thin fingers into what had given her the nickname "Claw." She slashed at the air. "All that clanging and smoky smell came from my imagination?"

Claudia looked out the window. A brick wall. That was all she saw.

Her counselor, a plain-faced woman without makeup, wore

brown, oversized glasses. "We call it mass hallucination. Common among malleable minds, especially your age. Caused by the excitement of the moment."

"And that costume and mask that looked like Trevor—" Claudia crossed her arms. "You're saying that guy wasn't a demon."

The woman shifted in her chair. "You know demons don't exist."

"What about my nightmares? Can't you help me?"

"Some time at New Peace Clinic might give you a new perspective."

Claudia bounced to her feet. "No, thanks. I'll be fine." She flashed her best fake smile. "Helps just to talk to you." She snatched her furry sweater from the back of the chair. "See you next week."

3

PATCH LIKED BEING up front with Snips. The guy listened as if he considered Patch an equal.

"Don't you wish everyone could see God's power? Think how that would change their minds."

The sun had set and Patch noticed they were skirting the highways in favor of small, two-lane roads. It took longer, but Patch didn't mind.

"That doesn't guarantee they'd believe," Snips said.

"But how could anyone see what we saw and not understand that angels and demons are duking it out? God exists even if people deny him."

"No need to convince me, Patch. I'm on your side." Patch thought Snips's eyes looked puffy. "I'm just saying that even when people stick their foot in a miracle, they don't necessarily believe."

"Like the Israelites."

"Exactly. Miracle after miracle, but they still turned on Moses."

"Well," Patch said, "I just want whatever God has for the Tattooed Rats and me. I can hardly wait to see where he sends us."

4

WANNA SEE MY lizard, Erin?" Terry said. She could not believe her parents had given him one of those slimy things for his fourth birthday. Reptiles gave her the creeps. But she didn't want to ruin her homecoming. Her parents had allowed her back into the house on the condition that she caused no problems. That she'd flip over a new leaf.

Erin was no longer a runaway like Patch.

She allowed herself to be dragged to her little brother's room, where she found a plastic T-rex, a dinosaur bedspread, and drawings of the same pinned to a large bulletin board. A classic boy's room.

She was glad to be home.

One crayon creation showed Terry holding hands with someone labeled P-A-T-C-H. Erin stared.

The boy snatched the lizard gently with two cupped hands. Erin looked at the dark, cold eyes. "Cuddly as a scorpion," she said.

Terry held the animal up to his nose. "Kinda looks like Trevor."

"What did you say?" Horrified, Erin dropped to her knees, facing her brother.

"That kid talked to Mommy lots while you were gone. He was always here. I didn't like him. He was scary without his mask."

"Terry, why was Trevor here?" Erin trembled but her voice stayed strong. She held Terry's small shoulders. Maybe he was making up a story. "Did he hurt you?"

"No." Terry tickled the lizard under the chin, and it flicked out a long tongue. "I'm not supposed to talk about it."

"And Mom knew?"

Terry looked surprised. "She invited him."

This response stiffened her spine. "What did *they* do?"

The boy crept closer and put his lips near her ear. "Talked while I napped. I listened sometimes." Guilt covered his face.

Erin knew it would be best to drop this, but she couldn't help herself. "What did they say?"

"Talked about you and Patch. Trevor wanted you . . . punished."

The word had come out, slowly, as if it were too big for the boy's mouth. Terry let the lizard scurry several inches before snatching it. "Scared me, so I stopped listening."

"You're sure he didn't hurt you?" Erin had to know.

The boy plopped the lizard back in its terrarium. "Nope. Said he wanted to be my friend." He kissed the lizard's head. "But I didn't believe him."

"And that's all that happened?" Erin squinted to make Terry see she was serious.

"Sure." Terry copied his lizard's expression, refusing to blink. "I already told you, Trevor scared me when he took off his mask.

He looked like that." He pointed to a raptor, one of his favorite dinos.

Well, Erin knew *that* had to be an exaggeration. But clearly there was something very different, very wrong about Trevor.

CLAUDIA WAS ANGRY. Why did she have to go to counseling? She hated sitting like a bug under a magnifying glass. Sometimes she just stared back, trying to annoy the unsmiling lady behind the desk.

Her troubles had started when she realized she could make serious money turning Patch in. She didn't have any trouble turning in a classmate. He was a Christ-Kid and deserved to be behind bars. Christians had no rights.

But she'd brought friends in to help, and the whole thing fell apart. They were not to be trusted. Not one of them. And now with Erin back, it was all too weird.

At least it was now summer break. She wouldn't have anything to do with them. She'd find a part-time job and spend every penny she made on herself. Her nails needed some work.

Almost falling in love with a demon had caused a lot of stress. What was with her, always getting involved with losers? She wouldn't let that happen again.

Her mom pounced the minute she got in the door. "How was the appointment?"

"Fine." Short answers drove her mother crazy.

"Any breakthroughs?"

"Nope." Claudia acted as though she hadn't a care in the world. She shut her bedroom door without a sound.

Though she wouldn't admit it to another soul, she did care what her mother thought. And she was worried.

Was she really seeing demon monsters?

And if so, why? No answers yet, despite staring down the counselor in three straight sessions.

Claudia contemplated her fingernails. They were getting long. Reminded her of . . .

Of course! Why hadn't she thought of going directly to the source? Claudia had to talk to Trevor, see if he could explain what she was seeing. Explain who or what had been inside that mask.

She wasn't prejudiced. Anyone could be her friend so long as they did her some good. She didn't much care if he was from heaven or hell as long as he provided answers. And maybe a whole lot more. Trevor could make the summer interesting if he was brave enough to show his human face around her again.

She had the dirt. And if he wanted any information about him kept quiet, he'd have to pay.

5

OKAY, I GIVE up," Patch said, uncovering his eyes and blinking at the harsh overhead lights. "Where are we?"

Laura walked with him. Snips clomped along behind.

A row of unfamiliar faces greeted him. He gladly took the outstretched hands. Some grabbed him, held him close like a long-lost friend. "Great to see you, man. Glad you're safe." Lots of tattoos but no one he knew. At least the long road trip was over.

"God protects," Patch said.

"Amen," said a chorus.

"Guess you were surprised to see the New Peace van," said one skinny man, his hair a red mop.

Who were these people?

"Prayer warriors," Snips said. "Praying for you for months."

"They don't know me from Adam."

"No matter." Snips clasped a man's hand.

"Feels good to be the one prayed for," Patch said. Laura nodded, her face pale. "Where are we?"

He zeroed in on a large map of the United States taped to a far wall. Video feeds, each marked with place and time, covered another.

On a tiny spot in the middle of Nevada a small sticker said, "You are here." Amusing.

"Hey, I'm starving."

"We've got plenty of food."

It was Gary, the long-haired leader of the Tattooed Rats.

Patch couldn't believe it. "Where have you been hiding?" The two hugged.

Gary was smiling but Patch thought he looked serious too. He didn't like the look in his eyes.

"Missed you, Patch Man. All the Rats have."

"Are others here?"

"None that you knew. All scattered after McCry's raid." Gary rubbed his hands together. "If not for you, man, a whole lot might have been thrown into prison."

"I bet Cheryl McCry wasn't too thrilled to find me gone." Patch thought of that night. Of the shattering battle between angels and demons.

Gary pointed to a chair. "Look, Patch, we know what you went through fighting off Trevor, dealing with McCry, so we don't want you to take this wrong."

Oh, brother. "We're friends. Just tell me." A familiar twinge sparked in his abdomen. Patch had hoped he was growing out of the ulcers. Maybe not.

His face must have shown his discomfort.

"Hurting again?" Gary said.

"I'm fine. Now, what? Give it to me straight."

"Okay, there's your health. We can never be sure when you'll relapse. We think the best thing would be for us to leave you here to rest up."

"I wanted to go with the Rats into the city to share Christ with kids."

"That's not what we want for you."

"Didn't know you could read God's mind," Patch said, letting irritation creep into his voice. "I thought you wanted help."

"We helped you escape, man." Gary put an arm around Patch, and it took all of Patch's self-control not to shrug it off. "Hide out awhile. McCry's not going to let you go easily."

Patch felt that pull in his gut, low and painful. "She's after me already?"

Gary unfolded a map and pointed to a dot.

"Demon's Bluff?" Patch said. "Sounds like a really hot place."

"Nevada is beautiful if you like cactus, pack rats, and rocks." He handed Patch the map. "When you're up to it, you're welcome to join the TRs. Meanwhile, you might find small-town living more exciting than you think."

ME? YOU'RE SURE?" Trevor gnawed his tail, using it to clean between his teeth. "No thanks. I'd rather work alone this time. No one in the way."

"Flabbygums said you would love the challenge of mentoring us. We wanted someone who's already a star." A female demon about his age scratched her green cheek. "We're your extra credit."

"Whatever." Trevor couldn't believe he'd have a couple losers huffing behind him learning his tricks. Not cool.

Demon Guy hid behind Demon Girl. Unlike her, he seemed afraid of Trevor. Good.

"The sooner I teach you my secrets the sooner I can send you back home." Trevor wished he had all the wisdom of death and destruction at his fingertips, but demons were notorious for refusing to help one another. He should know.

The female demon whistled appreciatively. "Some teeth, Trevor."

"Impressive, aren't they?" Trevor snapped his mouth shut, flicking his tail clear just in time. "So you want to learn the ways of the Wicked One. Guess I can share a few shortcuts to success in the human world."

"You're my hero," Demon Guy said finally.

"As I should be," Trevor said with a strut. "You two have a lot to learn to reach the next rank. Let me see your costumes."

The two slipped behind a screen and returned a minute later. The girl's hair was long, shiny brown, and tied in a ponytail. She wore a tank top, shorts, and pink tennis shoes. Ready to hit the high school cafeteria.

The boy had short, straight black hair and eyes dark as coal. He wore a ragged T-shirt bearing the name of a heavy-metal band. His jeans were bleached and tattered at the hems, and his shoes were white. Still looked kinda young—maybe only a freshman. But so what? It was all in the posing, the posturing, the patter.

Once they spent some quality time with him, they'd be able to imitate a human of any age. And know how to destroy one too.

Trevor stepped behind the screen and instantly came out the other side looking like a typical teen. "You'll learn to change faster.

Takes practice." He waved them closer. "Hang with me. I'll show you how to be the coolest teens around. You'll be my cousins from out of town."

Demon Girl was going to be a natural; she had a flair for drama. But Demon Guy was too shy. Of course some girls liked that "I'm all quiet and sensitive" look. At least that's what he heard from others.

Demons talked, gossiped. Just like their flesh-and-blood foes. That was one reason Trevor loved working with Claudia. They saw things the same.

Some said demons had no business taking on human form. Trevor didn't buy that. If angels could pretend to be humans once in a while, why not devils? Fair was fair. And people were gullible. Tricking them didn't take much.

Still, these two had a ways to go.

6

THE SIGN ANNOUNCED "Demon's Bluff: A Friendly Town. Population 2,980." The temperature at the bank read 113 degrees.

"Thanks, Gary," Patch said as he exited the car in front of the church. He tried to smile and wave as they left him there. Then he eyed the building in front of him. In the entryway was a bulletin board with a few stray notices. He added one saying he was a teen looking for summer work. He was sure to find something.

When he looked around he felt like he'd stepped back into some old TV show. A wide main street, lined with cacti, tied the downtown together. An old stone courthouse stood at the center, in the middle of a square. Signs said, "Keep off the grass." They were perched in gravel. Someone had a sense of humor.

A drugstore offered extra-thick malts. Sounded good to Patch. He was dying of thirst.

At the fire station, men and women scrubbed down a truck that looked more like a toy. One of the women sprayed the others. Patch wished he could cool off too.

Maybe he *would* grow to like this place.

Nearby, a corner grocery listed specials in white chalk. The grocer was stacking apples in a slanted box.

"New in town?"

Patch nodded. He might as well have a shirt that said "Not from here."

"Noticed you hangin' round that church." The man handed him a rosy apple and Patch thanked him. "We won't abide vandals. We're good, God-fearin' people."

Patch bit into the apple. "And you're not afraid to let people know?"

The man tucked a thumb into suspenders that covered a long-sleeved white shirt. "Know what?"

"About being a Christian."

The man clapped Patch's shoulder. "You must be from the city. We don't care about the World Peace Alliance and such nonsense. Not in the middle of nowhere."

"What about the police?" Across the street in front of the small brick stationhouse, two men in uniform sat playing checkers. "What if they turn you in?"

"Both of 'em sing in the choir," the grocer said, waving the officers over. Patch nearly bolted from instinct.

After the pleasantries, Patch found that the cops didn't mind that he was a Christian. No one did, because everyone was.

Yes, he might just like this place.

WHEN THE WHINY voice repeated her name, Claudia knew who it was without looking.

Nancy was the same—plain brown hair, plain brown clothes, and that ever-present know-it-all expression.

Claudia had no time for this. She was on a mission to find Trevor. "What do you want?"

"Wondered if you've seen Granger."

Hmm. Granger. Claudia checked off her list: too tall, skinny, awkward, and big nosed. Nancy could have him.

"I need to talk to him."

Lucky Granger, Claudia thought. "If I see him I'll let him know." She winked.

"It's not like that," Nancy said quickly.

"Like what?" Claudia loved watching her squirm.

I DON'T KNOW why you're upset." Mrs. Morgan looked away from her kitchen computer screen.

Erin wished her mom would pay attention. "Because you invited Trevor into the house. Weren't you afraid?"

"Why would I be? At least he has manners."

"Did Terry tell you about Trevor taking off his mask?"

Her mother gave her a look. "Little boys have big imaginations. So did you at that age."

"I don't trust him, Mom."

"Trevor was a great help to me when you took off with that hoodlum, Patrick Johnson. Even offered to find you. I don't know what I would have done without him." Mrs. Morgan lowered her voice. "Even your father liked him."

That *was* a surprise. If Daddy liked him, everyone must.

"Terry's playing games with you, Erin. Don't take him so seriously."

It was going to be one long summer.

7

THE WOMAN POINTED at Patch's shoulder bag. "That all you have?"

"The Bible says to travel light," he said. He didn't want her to know that he was indeed carrying everything he owned.

"Very true. Well, Omar and I could use some help this summer. Seems God sent you our way."

The woman sure seemed nice. Her mostly gray hair was long and straight. Her dark skin was etched with wrinkles, but Patch still thought she was pretty. She wore a white, short-sleeved shirt, jeans, and a brown western hat.

She pointed to a beat-up red pickup. Patch hopped in and enjoyed the rural scenery and the clear blue Nevada sky as they drove toward her house. He could rest here, maybe start forgetting the mistakes he'd made—and remembering the good times with his mom and dad, with his little sister Jenny. They were gone and it still hurt.

A long dirt road led to the small, single-story home. Once there, a boy on crutches came to the door and smiled at Patch. The boy wore denim suspenders and dusty boots. "Soup's ready, Ma."

When the boy reached for Patch's bag, Patch said, "Thanks, I got it."

"Hey, I do my fair share around here. And if I want to show you some hospitality, don't begrudge me."

"Thanks." Patch handed him the bag and introduced himself.

The boy nodded. "Jarrod. Glad you're here." He held the door for his mom and Patch. His darker skin matched his mom's.

She sniffed. "Lamb stew? My favorite."

"You'll be bunking with me," Jarrod said. "In the back, next to the bathroom."

8

WHAT DO YOU think I am, a dating service?" Claudia shoved back a swatch of her thick hair. "I don't know where Nancy is, Granger. But I do know she was looking for you."

They had run into each other at a park with bike paths, a pond, and a gray stone fountain. It was a sunny California day.

"You mean that?" Granger looked both eager and pathetic.

Claudia wished she could whack some sense into him. "Why don't you go sit by the fountain. If I see Nancy, I'll send her your way."

Granger sat and Claudia waved good-bye.

If I see Nancy I'll tell her Granger said he'd meet her at the mall. Maybe I'm a dating service after all. Just not a good one.

TREVOR STRODE ALONG the sidewalk with his two protégés. Their assignment was to spot Claudia from his description. Encased in their disguises, they were failing miserably, choosing wrong, then missing her when she did show up. He wondered if they both needed glasses.

He saw big golden earrings jangling like wind chimes and waved. "Here she comes. I'd know that glare anywhere. Hey, Claw!" He liked the way her shoulders pulled back at his voice, as if he'd scraped a chalkboard with sharp nails.

"Trevor. I didn't know the circus was in town." She pointed to the two trailing him. "Clown hunting? I see you've found two already."

"You were right, Trevor." The girl crossed her arms. "I'm Hope. Pretty name, huh?"

Claudia ignored her.

"She's beautiful even if she is mean," the teen boy said. "You can call me Barry." He took off his cap and mashed it in his hands, lowered his eyes.

Not bad. He almost looked cool. Trevor was impressed. The kid had been listening to his instructions.

"Smarter than he looks. Polite too." Claudia nuzzled Trevor's shoulder, her back to the others. "I want to make a deal with you."

P ATCH LIKED THAT the family prayed before they ate. They were also polite and civil to each other.

Jarrod's left shoulder jutted awkwardly. His crutches rested on the back of his chair. He had no appetite problems. He gulped the soup.

"You and Jarrod can fix some fence this afternoon," the father said. "If it's not the animals, it's the wind."

"Sometimes it blows through like the devil's breath," Jarrod said.

"Demon's Bluff can be rough," Jarrod's mother said. "But we get by."

"I'll keep watch over him," Jarrod said. Patch caught his warning look.

Patch finished off a second glass of milk. "You like that?" Jarrod's mom said.

"Tastes different from the store stuff."

"That's because it's from our goat."

9

"YOU DON'T KNOW what you're asking." Trevor kept his voice low.

"You want privacy," Claudia said. "I want information."

Claudia could see she had the upper hand. Trevor looked nervously at his cousins. "And all you want is before-the-fact knowledge? I guess that's not asking much." He smiled, showing off his perfect white teeth. Too perfect.

Claudia figured something was weird about the two kids as well, but she didn't care.

"I ask, you answer. No matter the question, no matter the topic."

"Deal." He held out a hand, and Claudia took it in both of hers. "If you're sure that's what you want. And you'll keep my secret."

Claudia nodded, grinning. "Hey. We all wear masks." Claudia looked Trevor up and down. Blond hair, dark blue eyes, model looks. "Some fit better than others."

"Here," Trevor said. "Something to seal the deal." He gave her a necklace. The chain was thin with a circular backdrop depicting a bird with wings wide and talons open.

"Scary." Claudia pretended to gnaw on it. "Tastes like silver."

"Nothing but the best for my girl. It can be used as a walkie-talkie—among other things. You need me, you grab the necklace and call. Simple as that."

"All I have to do is hold the necklace?"

"And I'll be at your side in a flash," Trevor said, "telling you whatever you need to know."

Claudia fingered the round medallion. "I don't believe you."

"Claw. Have I ever lied? I mean, to you?"

"Let's try it," she said. "Out of the way, annoying ones." She hurried past Trevor's cousins and around the corner. Out of sight, but would that also mean out of mind?

When she squeezed the charm, her hair lifted at the back of her neck and a tingle ran through her arms. "Speak to me, Trevor."

Nothing.

"Thought he said he'd be at my side," she muttered.

I am, Claudia. But closer.

That was crystal clear, loud, hardwired to her brain. Trevor was at least a block away and around the corner, but his essence was with her. Claudia couldn't have explained it if she tried, but this was like having a personal genie.

And she liked it.

MOLLY," ERIN SAID. "Want to come in?"

Molly looked uncomfortable, scared. "I didn't know if you'd even talk to me."

"Hey, things happen. We move on." Erin pointed to a chair.

Molly entered, flipping her ponytail back. "I want to ask you about the night Patch left."

"I don't think that's a good idea."

Molly took Erin's hand. "Did he really give himself up for the rest of you?"

Erin nodded slowly. How could she explain seeing her friend thrown to the concrete, beaten, kidnapped, while she didn't lift a finger. She'd just run, happy to escape.

Erin told Molly everything—all about the prayers, the Tattooed Rats, the war in the skies and streets, angels battling demons.

"I didn't think Patch had it in him."

"He was brave." Erin was surprised at her own defensiveness. "I liked him. And now he's going to be McCry's walking, talking advertisement for the power of mind control."

They sat a moment, considering what that meant. Then Erin sighed.

"Sometimes I feel like Patch ruined my life." She refilled Molly's Coke. "If he hadn't come around, I wouldn't know what I was missing, wouldn't long for something more."

"Exactly," Molly said. "I can't ever go back to not knowing, not caring."

"And that's why we hate him." Erin bit into a pretzel.

Molly grinned. "Pretty lame, huh?"

"Instead of thanking him for yanking our blinders off, we're annoyed that we have to think."

They laughed.

"We owe Patch, Molly," Erin said. "We ought to try to visit him."

Molly put her glass on the kitchen counter. "We have to find out where they're keeping him. Even killers on death row are allowed visitors. It's not like he's dangerous."

The two sat together before the computer, searching for stories about the capture of Patrick Johnson. Not much available. They found a report announcing that he would serve the WPA as a spokesman to youth: "Thanks to Cheryl McCry for allowing me to do something worthwhile with my life, to share the message that only tolerance can bring peace." That didn't sound like him.

"Look at that," Molly said, leaning close to the screen. "Patch is waving with his left hand."

"And he's right handed. Maybe the picture has been reversed."

"Look closer. The sign on that building in the background isn't backwards."

"I'll bet his left-handed wave is Patch's way of crossing his fingers."

"Or a fake," Molly said.

They searched for more, but nothing came up. "That's where the trail ends," Erin said. "Patch all of a sudden disappears from the news."

"I thought he was supposed to be the new face of peace," Molly said, "telling kids how tolerance is the only path to truth. Where are the ads, TV clips, pop-ups?"

"Maybe they're torturing him."

"Or he's escaped."

"But how?" Erin said. "I saw McCry's goons beat him and throw him in a van."

"Patch always said that God works in weird ways."

Not as easy as I thought it would be," Patch said, sweating, ready for a break, maybe some dinner.

"We don't stop working till Dad does," Jarrod said.

His father was moving steady as an ox, not even breathing hard. Jarrod tossed Patch the canteen.

"What did your mother mean when she said Demon's Bluff could be hard?"

Jarrod's father trudged toward the house, so the boys leaned on the fence. "At the end of every summer," Jarrod said, "right before harvest, the Demon's Bluff Spirit Fest brings visitors. Some worship Satan—to inhale the 'demon's breath,' his essence. Others hang out on the courthouse square, stomping the gravel and littering while waiting for the next band."

"Why doesn't anybody stop them?"

"It's a free country. We can't keep them from packing the parks, chanting, dancing."

That didn't sound so scary. He wanted to hear more. "And . . . ?"

Jarrod tugged on his old ball cap. "They summon the darkness. I've heard, but I haven't seen it for myself."

"Seen what?"

"They say the breath of Satan fills the night—a screaming, tearing, roaring sound that rolls over Demon's Bluff, the ledge overlooking the valley." Jarrod scratched his twisted shoulder. "You don't want to be out on that night. People disappear."

"I still don't see why the people of Demon's Bluff allow it."

"No choice. 'Sides, folks sell a whole lot of pies, quilts, wooden toys. Good business. That's what my dad says."

Patch had to think about that. Was it right to make money off people who came to worship evil? "I just don't get how you can just stand around and let it happen year after year." He paced.

"Calm down," Jarrod said. He jammed his cap back on his head. "You're making way too much of this. It's not like they're vandals. I mean, yeah, they leave a mess, but just because we let 'em hang around for a long weekend doesn't mean we agree with them." Jarrod turned and pounded a nail, his back to Patch.

"Think how people could be misled," Patch said. Jarrod kept working. "What if you had a little brother who didn't see anything wrong with it? I wouldn't care how many of my mother's quilts they bought. I wouldn't want them around."

They slipped a heavy post into a hole. Jarrod paused and looked at him. "You've got a point, Patch. Those people do give me the creeps."

10

"Hey, Granger," Claudia said, pouting. "Nancy never showed?"

"Nope." The back of his neck was sunburned. He rose to leave the park.

Claudia surreptitiously gripped the medallion. "Hold on a second. I want to help."

Granger stopped and crossed his arms.

Is Granger really into Nancy? Claudia wondered.

He wants to know if she's been seeing demons like he has, Trevor's voice said.

"Really?" Claudia said aloud.

"Really what?" Granger said. "You all right?"

"Yeah, sorry. Um, I've been wondering whether Nancy has seen the same demons we have."

Granger went pale and clearly struggled for words. "You too?"

"It's okay, Granger." She beckoned him with a forefinger and put her lips to his ear. "It's a special ability only intelligent kids have."

Granger looked scared.

"Ask Nancy," Claudia said. "She'll tell you. Everyone with inner vision can see those creatures. Some say they're evil, but who are we to judge?" She jangled an earring with her finger.

"What are you talking about? They tried to kill me. My dad nearly pulled the plug on me because those things made it look like I was in a coma."

"Don't be so narrow-minded. Just because you don't understand something doesn't mean it's wrong."

Claudia squeezed the necklace ornament, willing Trevor to return.

That was fun, she said silently.

Welcome to my world. Who's next?

Nancy.

Your wish is my command, Trevor said, a smirk in his tone.

PATCH HADN'T BEEN inside a church in years and never a full one. He had enjoyed the service, but now he sat fidgeting. Jarrod had persuaded Pastor Ron to let Patch bring a few words of greeting as a newcomer.

Jarrod introduced him, saying, "He's been talking to me about the Demon's Bluff Spirit Fest."

Patch stepped up. "This is a great town," he said to polite applause. He wanted these people on his side. "And Jarrod and his parents are some of the kindest Christians I've ever met." Patch paused. "But your town has a bad reputation."

Heads jerked up all over the sanctuary, and the pastor stood. "What are you talking about, young man?"

"The Spirit Fest is wicked. Period. You're allowing people here who could pollute the minds of children. We need to take a stand against evil."

"Is that all?" someone shouted.

Pastor Ron laughed as he approached. "I'm sorry if we made you late for your dinners. This youngster's faith just needs to grow a little. You're dismissed."

Patch trudged from the pulpit as people glared and nudged each other. Jarrod caught up with him, deftly using his crutches. "It was worth a try, Patch. But there are other ways to get the word out."

Outside, Patch was relieved to see Jarrod had not, apparently, lost any friends over the pulpit fiasco. He was surrounded by other kids as they left the church. Patch wondered what it would be like to have people look at him that way.

"Patch helped me see the dangers," Jarrod said, as a dozen friends hung on every word. "If the adults won't do anything, we should."

A tall boy with a shock of blond hair said, "What's the big deal? My family sells a bunch of jerky every summer. Helps us buy clothes for school." He pointed to his too-short jeans. "Due for a new pair." Everyone laughed.

Jarrod held up a hand. "Let Patch have his say."

The kids sure acted more open than the adults had. "I'm new to this place," he said. "I see people who care about each other and who seem to care about their kids. But with this Spirit Fest, they're allowing in more than jerky buyers and people who want a deal on a quilt. All I'm saying is that we should think twice about all this. It could be dangerous. Think about your younger brothers and sisters. They're the ones I worry about. They need to know it's wrong to call on the devil and ask him to breathe power into them."

11

SHE DIDN'T FEEL at home among floor-to-ceiling books. Yuck. But this was where Trevor had said Claudia would find Nancy. He was right. There she was at the Special Order counter.

Claudia put her arm around Nancy's thin waist. "I've been looking all over for you."

"You have?"

"Of course. With school out, I have more time for the people I care about." Claudia looked Nancy over. The girl needed to put on some weight, maybe try a little eyeliner and lipstick.

Nancy's lip trembled.

Good. She was buying this baloney. Claudia smiled.

"Thanks. I haven't run into anyone else from the old gang."

"Well, Marty's at military camp all summer learning the mysterious ways of the WPA. And the teachers are under sedation."

Nancy shot her a double take. "A joke," Claudia said softly. "And Granger's been around."

Nancy's eyes brightened. "He has?"

How does she feel about him, Trevor? I mean, really?

She's got it bad. Thinks she loves the guy.

"Yeah," Claudia said. "He's such a nice guy. And handsome." She hid the fact that the words almost made her gag. "I was thrilled when he asked me out." She popped open her compact and checked her lip liner.

Nancy's jaw dropped. "He did?"

"I'm looking forward to seeing him all summer."

Nancy looked devastated. "Good to see you, Claw," she said flatly. "I gotta run."

It doesn't get better than this.

Trevor didn't respond. He didn't have to.

JARROD HOBBLED ALONG as he and Patch left the farmhouse and headed for Demon's Bluff. When they came within view, he used a crutch as a pointer. "That's where it all happens."

The rise, lit by the setting sun, consisted of a rocky table extending to a drop-off—an oasis of beauty in the harsh desert.

"As long as they're coming anyway," Patch said, "we ought to be ready for them."

Jarrod squinted. "Meaning?"

"Plan an event of our own, maybe a prayer rally. If it bothers them, they won't be back. But if they listen, who knows what might happen?"

"What about my parents, Pastor Ron, the others? I don't think they see the need."

"They can't nix a prayer rally, can they?"

They moseyed around the whole area. Cacti towered over scrub trees with tiny leaves. A breeze bent the wildflowers. Patch was convinced this place should tell people of God's creation, not serve as a backdrop for evil.

12

CLAUDIA LED GRANGER into her weedy backyard where they sat on lawn chairs beneath a tree. He looked serious. "I still want to know how you knew."

"I told you. I've seen them too." She couldn't get over how skinny Granger's neck was.

"But you thought everyone would think you were crazy. I know the feeling."

Claudia had conspired with Trevor. She knew what to say. "I believe these beings mean us no harm." She looked down at the shining tips of her long blonde hair.

"But they held me down. Made it look like I was in a coma."

Claudia shook her head and touched Granger's arm. "You don't understand. They were afraid. They didn't know you were on their side."

Granger looked away. "We can be on their side?" Clearly, the thought surprised him.

"Of course. They want to guide us. They can be helpful if you know how to use them."

"I could use some help." He stood. "I've got lots of questions."

Claudia reached into her pocket and squeezed the medallion. *Can we give him access too?*

You sure you want to do that? You won't be the only one on the block with the gift.

That was all right with her. "Can you keep a secret, Granger?"

"Sure. What?"

"I want to show you how you can get in touch with something wise women and men have known about for ages."

He looked spooked, ready to leave. "Slow down, Claw," he said. "I don't want to get into anything weird."

Check your other pocket, Trevor said.

She pulled out a heavy ring.

Offer it to him. Same deal as you.

"See this?" Claudia rolled it in her palm, examining the engraving of the same bird that graced her necklace. "Try it on."

"It's awesome," he said. "And it fits like it was made for me."

"Now rub it with your thumb. No, with the thumb on your other hand. Yeah, like that."

Granger's eyes grew wide. "I hear her."

"Her?" Claudia hadn't expected that.

"A voice, telling me to ask any questions. She says she'll tell me whatever I want to know."

"Ask her what I'm thinking."

Granger blushed. "What is Claudia thinking?"

Claudia put her hands on Granger's shoulders and kissed him on the lips. "See? Was she right?"

Granger yanked the ring from his finger and tossed it in the grass. "That's creepy." With a shudder, he walked away.

"There's nothing to be afraid of," Claudia called after him. "And that's the last kiss you'll get from me."

As always, Cheryl McCry wore black. Like a witch. But rather than a tall pointy hat, she wore a scarf around her neck, a tight-fitting jacket, and a short skirt. Erin saw no cat, but the woman did have a bobble-head frog on her desk.

Molly tapped it and watched the head wiggle. Erin wondered if this visit had been a bad idea.

"So you want to see our prisoner?" McCry tapped on her keyboard and spun the monitor to face the girls.

"He was our friend," Molly said.

"So you're here to gloat."

Erin scrunched up her nose, and Molly scowled.

The screen showed Patch against a pale blue wall, standing tall. "I don't understand," Erin said.

"Um-hm. So you're not here to rub it in my face." McCry fingered an ebony bow at her neck.

"Rub what in your—"

McCry tapped a long fingernail on the screen. "Escaped. At large. Considered dangerous."

The girls exchanged glances. "We didn't know," Molly said. "It hasn't been on the news, and—"

"Nevertheless, I'm glad you dropped in," McCry said. "We don't have tours here."

"No." Molly said. "He's a friend. We wanted to cheer him up."

"If you expect me to believe that—" She cut herself off and stood. "We're through here. But, girls, if you happen to hear from Patrick Johnson, let me know immediately. I'll know if you don't, and I'll send my friends to visit *you*."

13

GRANGER FINALLY CAUGHT up with Nancy as she approached her house with an armload of books.

"I've been looking for you."

"Hey." Nancy didn't stop walking.

After what they'd been through, Granger thought she'd be happier to see him.

"You're not going to believe what Claudia said," he said.

She kept her distance. "Maybe I will."

"She's seen them too."

Nancy stopped. "Seen what?"

Granger looked from side to side. "You know. The things. The creatures."

She started moving again. "I have no idea what you're talking about. But I understand you and Claudia have decided to take your friendship to the next level."

Why was she acting this way? And how could she know?

"Hey, she kissed me, not the other way around."

That stopped her again. She turned and faced him. "I was talking about you two going out. You're kissing already?"

"Going out?" Granger felt as if he were sinking. So she hadn't seen the kiss?

Nancy shook her head, and her face flushed like she was about to cry. Granger wanted to run. Where had Nancy gotten the idea he was going out with the Claw? That was crazy.

"I'm sorry," was all he could manage.

JUST MINUTES AFTER Nancy slammed her door in Granger's face, the doorbell rang. Couldn't he take a hint?

But it was Claudia, blonde and bouncy. "What's wrong, Nance?"

"Leave me alone," Nancy said, trying to close the door.

Claudia pushed her way in. "Look, can't we talk about this?"

"About what?"

"I don't like to see my friends hurting."

That was a laugh. To Nancy it seemed Claudia lived for this.

"It wasn't Granger's fault anyway. This thing is to blame." Claudia opened her hand.

"A ring?"

"Slip it on and you'll see. Granger didn't use it right."

Claudia pressed the ring into Nancy's palm. Nancy felt the warmth and saw the glow. Claudia pulled her outside onto the front porch.

Nancy put it on. "This couldn't have been Granger's. It fits me perfectly."

Claudia urged her on. "It looks great, Nancy. Now just open your mind and ask any question you want, and your spirit will guide you to the answer."

"That's crazy," Nancy said, rolling her eyes.

14

WHEN CLAUDIA GOT home, Granger was waiting for her.

"What'd you tell Nancy?" he said.

"You mean about us?"

Granger looked like he wanted to slug someone. "There is no us. Now what's going on?"

"You want to deny the truth? I know Nancy hates dealing with reality; I didn't know you did. Yeah, I told her we kissed. So what? I'm trying to help you two communicate better, that's all. I didn't mean to cause trouble." She slipped her hand into Granger's. "It was only a kiss."

"How do I explain that to her?"

Claudia stroked Granger's jaw. "Don't bother. She should trust you."

"I wish she would. I like her."

"Me too. That's why I want to help. And here, you dropped

this." She had left the original ring with Nancy, but he didn't have to know she had a spare.

"I don't want anything to do with that."

"Fine." Claudia tossed it into the air. "But Nancy sure likes hers." Granger caught the ring before it hit the floor. "She has one?"

"Yup. When she heard you did, she wanted one for herself."

"But when I asked her about those things we were both seeing, she pretended to have no clue what I was talking about." Granger turned the ring over, tracing the image with his finger. "This thing freaked me out."

"Practice makes perfect."

TREVOR STOOD BEFORE McCry and her computer, his blond hair spiky and gelled. He wore a long, sloppy shirt. He felt cool.

"I don't know." McCry opened another screen. "Last time you disappeared when I needed you most."

"Well, I'm back, and it's time."

"Great." She didn't sound sincere.

"This will work. And it'll scare him too." Trevor tapped his skull. "I've thought this out."

"So have I." McCry yanked a sheet from the printer and scribbled her name. "This will authorize the search. Anyone harboring Patrick Johnson will have quite the motivation to turn him in."

Trevor read the poster before stuffing it in his pocket. "Fifty thousand is a lot of money. Not sure he's worth that."

"He's not. But we won't tell anyone that until they try to collect."

"Since you're not capable of finding him, ma'am, this is our only hope."

"That's what I like about you, Trevor—the way you work so well with others."

He bounded from her office. Once word got out about the reward, she would be flooded with calls. All he had to do was wait.

$$ $$

BAD NEWS, PATCH," Jarrod's dad said, sliding a rumpled sheet of paper across the table to him and Jarrod. "Pastor received this on the fax early this morning."

"Fifty thousand! I should turn my*self* in."

"That could pay for a lot of things around here," Jarrod's dad said. "But you don't have to worry about us or anyone else in this town. You're part of us now, and we stick by our own."

Patch wasn't so sure. And he had just started to feel comfortable. "That's a lot of money, Jarrod. Why shouldn't you turn me in?"

Jarrod's expression made Patch feel terrible. "We're poor, but I would never hurt a friend." Jarrod turned away.

"I'm sorry," Patch said. "I didn't mean it. Just scared, I guess."

"Me too. But promise you'll trust me, man. I won't let you down."

Patch nodded. He could do that for now. He had other plans anyway. He'd already contacted the Tattooed Rats about getting out. If things went right, he'd be gone soon. Before Jarrod or anyone else in Demon's Bluff changed their minds.

And there was that phone number deep in his wallet. He could always call Erin.

15

NANCY RUBBED THE ring. *What about the mail lady? What's her story?* She had to know. Okay, she was hooked.

A young girl's voice told her everything about the woman. This was great—reading minds, hearing thoughts, knowing all. Way too much fun.

Nancy ran to the mailbox. "Sorry about your cat."

The woman looked up, clearly surprised. "How'd you know?"

"You didn't seem yourself. Theresa was a good friend, wasn't she? A Siamese, right?"

Tears came to the woman's heavy eyes. "Like one of my babies."

"Thinking of getting another? I'm sure you provide a wonderful home."

The woman smiled. "I do, and you're right, I probably should. I'm glad you came to get your mail this morning."

I could get used to this. Her parents were next. Nancy couldn't wait to tap into them for a while.

I'M SCARED," MOLLY said over the phone.

"Me too." Erin took a deep breath. Things were happening too fast. "Ads online, on TV, everywhere, all about Patch."

"And a lot of people would do just about anything for that kind of money."

Erin used to think Molly was one of those people, willing to sell out a friend. She asked what Molly wanted to do.

"Go with you."

Erin liked the idea. Strength in numbers, especially when you're afraid. "Okay. They can get zero information from both of us as easily as one."

"You don't know where Patch is, do you?" Molly said. "Tell me if you do."

Could Erin really trust a girl like Molly? "No idea. Not a word from him."

"So we'll go face McCry together again. It's not like we're being called to testify in court."

"Nope," Erin said. "This is worse."

16

GRANGER SPUN THE ring slowly on his finger. What was wrong with using it? It worked, didn't it? Why not help himself to some information?

He'd try one more time, even if he did feel goofy, like he was rubbing a magic lamp.

Hey, Granger here.

A woman's sharp voice. *I know who you are.*

He didn't like her tone. *Just what I need. A smart-aleck spirit guide.*

I heard that. The sound of an irritated throat clearing, like an old lady with a cold, filled his head. Weird. Like someone running through your mind.

Do you have a question or not?

Yeah. Claudia. I want to know about the Claw.

Ask and I'll answer. The voice sounded resigned.

Did she really see demons? Granger wondered what was taking so long. *Hello, anyone home?*

Of course she didn't. Evil exists only in your mind. Claudia hasn't seen demons and neither have you.

That proved it. The ring could lie. Granger realized that when the voice in his head claimed demons were imaginary. He knew better.

So why the lie?

Granger wanted to figure this one out.

He would test it once more, ask about Nancy, see whether it was accurate. If it wasn't, he'd trash the ring.

This time there was no response. Maybe the speaker in his skull had tuned out. Yeah, that must be it.

Funny how his thoughts kept slipping to Nancy, to her smile and the tiny nose she claimed to hate.

Granger rubbed the cold metal and felt the power. He'd ask a different question this time.

Does Nancy like me? The very question embarrassed him, and he realized it wasn't a test at all; he really wanted to know. But how would he be able to tell whether the answer was true or not?

She adores you. Thinks about you constantly. Wishes you could work things out.

Granger hoped the voice was telling the truth this time. Of course, only Nancy could confirm it. He had to be man enough to ask her.

Suddenly he wanted to be rid of the ring. He yanked, but it wouldn't budge. He tried and tried but it was stuck. He would have to cut it off.

He held the ring up to the light and was struck anew by what a nice-looking piece of silver it was. Maybe he would keep it. Yeah.

As far as he knew, only two other people owned such a treasure. And Nancy was one of them. What could be better than that?

Nancy LOOKED AT herself in the mirror. Maybe she had a thing for Granger, but with her bright brown eyes and big smile, who needed him? She'd never looked happier, more alert. There was something about having a window into someone else's soul.

She hadn't seen even the shadow of a demon for days. Maybe she had imagined the one that leaped into her swimming pool or stuck claws into her friends.

Of course. She had created the whole thing in her mind. She sat in the living room with *Little Women* in her lap. Lame entertainment compared to the ring, but she would pretend in case her parents emerged from the bedroom where they seemed to be arguing.

The ring felt warm and tremors shook her hand as she rubbed it. Peace washed over her, and she liked the sensation.

Yes, Nancy?

Strange, that was the first time the voice had used her name.

Of course, I know your name. You're my friend, Nancy, and I'm always available whenever you call.

Give me something about my parents.

They're in their bedroom trying to keep quiet. They're angry.

With me?

Why would they be?

At what then?

At each other. They've tried everything.

Nancy tried to block the obvious question in her mind. Too late.

That's right, Nancy. They're getting a divorce.

17

CHERYL MCCRY LOOKS *weird,* Erin thought. Her silver hair had been dyed bright red and she wore lipstick to match. And bye-bye to black. Her clothes shone deep jungle green and her new scarf shimmered like emeralds.

Molly gave her a look, and Erin knew they were thinking the same thing: the makeover didn't work. Molly looked like she was having trouble keeping her laughter under control.

McCry held out a long hand, dainty as a princess. "Thanks for coming in again. Nice seeing you."

"Red's my brother's favorite color," Erin said.

"How *is* the little devil?" McCry put her hand over her mouth. "There I go again, speaking first, thinking second."

Erin remembered that McCry had talked with her mom and met Terry. Small world. Small, scary world.

"Please tell us where Patch is." Blunt, to the point. Erin hoped it might work. "You know, don't you?"

"Ladies, I want to be your friend." McCry came from behind her desk and crouched between the girls, a hand on each. She must have seen their shocked expressions. "I've been told I need to soften my approach."

Erin fought to keep from giggling. The woman who scared the socks off everyone now wanted to come across kind and gentle.

"I've kind of got plenty of friends," Erin said. "But thanks."

"Oh, I know that." McCry said. "It's Patrick Johnson—Patch to *his* friends—I'm particularly interested in."

"We haven't heard from him," Molly said.

"That's why we're here." Erin didn't like the way the conversation had turned.

McCry's eyes narrowed to silver slits. "That's what I expected you to say. But, hey, don't say I didn't try to be nice." Her hands went up in a shrug.

Erin stood to go, and Molly followed. When she opened the door a man was standing there.

"Bobby will escort you downstairs," McCry said, giving him a slow nod. "For the record, I tried the nice approach."

Bobby quickly slipped plastic restraints over Erin and Molly's wrists.

"What're you doing?" Erin said. "We don't know anything!"

McCry stuck out her lower lip. "If that's true, the interrogators will verify it and you have nothing to worry about. Use the serum, Bobby, and let me know."

The plastic dug into Erin's skin. "Pray, Molly. Pray," she said.

Before they could even fight back, the girls were dragged to a room with two beds, where they were tied down. A nurse flicked the tip of a hypodermic needle and plunged it into Erin's arm. The warm fluid tickled at first, then stung.

"Ouch!" Molly hollered. "Fight, Erin. Fight to stay . . . in . . . control . . ." She was already slurring. In seconds, her eyes fluttered, and she was gone.

Erin's thoughts rolled more and more slowly. Keeping her eyes open became a chore. "Please God, protect us."

Erin saw McCry in a small glassed-in room above the beds. She pointed, mouth moving in slow motion.

Erin's ears pounded and pain rose in her neck. The room began to swim.

18

PATCH WISHED HE could dig a hole and climb in. It had felt like Pastor Ron targeted him in the service that morning.

"Folks, we have a leaky roof, and we need money to fix it. If any of you can think of a way to come up with the cash, let me know." He had looked directly at Patch, and the chill was still with him.

After lunch, Jarrod sat next to him. "Sorry you haven't heard back from the Tattooed Rats."

Patch appreciated Jarrod's empathy.

"I don't get it," Patch said. "I thought they were my friends, that they'd do anything for me."

"There's probably a good reason. You'll know eventually."

Patch appreciated Jarrod's efforts. "Maybe they saw the ads and want to keep their distance. If they were thinking, they'd turn me in and take the cash. Wouldn't be the first time someone sold me out."

"Don't turn on everybody," Jarrod said. "Give us some credit."

"I'm not worried about you," Patch said.

"And you shouldn't worry about Pastor Ron either. He doesn't always get everything right, but I can hear God through him."

"I'll have to take your word for that."

Patch found himself wondering whether Erin might talk to him. Did she ever think of him? Yeah, just what she needed. Crazy Patch back in her life.

Patch knew he was poor company when Jarrod hobbled from the room. "Sorry, man," he called after him. "I'll be all right."

Erin was worth a try.

NANCY REALIZED THE very thought of divorce should have made her sad, but knowing before they told her was kind of cool. Other kids survived. And her parents had never seemed happy.

Nancy slipped into the living room where her mother had scads of yarn piled in a basket.

"So when were you and Dad planning on telling me about the divorce?"

Her mother froze. "What in the world . . . ?"

"I could tell something was wrong."

Her mother's knitting needles clattered to the floor. "Your father thinks a new arrangement will be for the best after all we've been through. But divorce? Where did you get that idea?"

"It's not true?" Impossible. Why would her voice make a mistake?

"Never. We decided you need to be sent to a special school, a camp for girls like you."

"Like me?" Nancy said.

"Who can't tell truth from lies. Remember when you pretended to see demons in our pool? And then all the trouble with that Patrick boy." She shook her head, her eyes clear and cold. "It's for the best."

"You saw them too." But it was obvious her parents had made up their minds.

"I don't know what you're talking about, dear," her mother said, winking. "I'm not the crazy one."

This wasn't working at all as Nancy had hoped. Her parents weren't divorcing each other. They were divorcing her. Boot camp was not how she wanted to spend her summer vacation.

What was with this stupid ring?

But no way was it budging over her knuckle. It warmed as she turned it.

Need something, Nancy?

"Shut up! Stop it! Get out of my head!"

Ask a question. Your wish is my command. The voice dripped with phony concern.

"Shut up! And I mean it! Mom, make the voice stop!"

But Nancy's mother backed out of the room.

Stay calm. I'm here to help.

"Liar! My mother thinks I'm crazy!"

Oh, no doubt, the voice said, laughing.

19

IF YOU'RE TRYING to reach Erin Morgan and aren't trying to sell me some junk, leave a message."

She sounded happy. Maybe it would be best to leave her alone.

He waited, unsure what to say. "Hey Erin, it's me . . ." was all Patch got out before the harsh click.

Probably for the best. She didn't need him back in her life.

ERIN FLEW LIKE Superman. None of that flapping like a bird; she was a rocket through a starry sky. No one could stop her.

She loved the freedom.

But then lightning struck close, filling her nose and mouth with ozone. Still, she didn't want to land, didn't want to stop.

"Erin, you know, don't you?" The voice was caring, mellow. "You can tell us. It's all right."

Something tugged at her arm, pulled at her skin. Hurt.

"Patrick Johnson. Patch. Where is he?"

"Gone." It took all her effort to focus, desperate to pry her eyes open. "Not here."

"That we know." Strong fingers pinched her shoulder, poking a pressure point that made her want to scream. "We need him."

Erin rubbed her eyes. She was too tired even to cry; she could only listen.

"Both girls say the same thing. I don't think they know. Get them out of here."

"You want us to drop them off?" The second person sounded nice.

"Sure, and why don't you get them ice cream too," McCry asked.

Erin's throat felt parched. Ice cream sounded good.

"They got here under their own power; send them home the same way." McCry hurried from the room.

"Yes, Ms. McCry." The voice lowered, "I mean, Ms. McClown." Erin burst out laughing, met the nurse's eyes, and they both smiled. Clearly, the other woman was no McCry fan either. She unlatched the restraints.

20

WELL, WELL." GRANGER checked out the flyer stapled to the telephone pole. He'd seen these all over town, plus heard radio spots, seen ads online and on TV. "Too bad we don't know where Patch is."

He spun the ring slowly. He could ask the voice where Patch was and use the reward to buy a killer car. It was about time he started thinking of himself. Forget Nancy. He'd tried to be nice to her.

Forget her. The voice was soft, kind. *She's already forgotten you.*

The ring got that right, even if it sometimes provided flaky information.

He pulled out his phone and dialed. "Hey, Claudia. Got time to talk?"

Her laughter went on too long. "Always plenty for my bestest and closest friend."

Granger knew she didn't mean it, but he didn't mind. He fingered his sunglasses back on his nose.

"I've got a deal in mind, a way to make up for missing out on the big reward last time."

"Patch?"

"You've seen the posters too?"

"Oh, yeah," she said. "And I think I know how we can find him."

So what if the ring sent mixed messages, especially about Nancy? Granger had the feeling that this time it would be right on the money.

L ET ME LISTEN again." Molly pushed play. "The first one sounded like Patch, but who is Jarrod?"

Erin shrugged. "Never heard of him. Says he's a friend of Patch's."

"Sure acted eager for you to come to Patch's rescue."

"That Demon's Bluff Spirit Fest sounds wild." Erin doubted she could get permission.

"My parents went before they were married." Molly pretended to gag.

"You've got to be kidding." Erin giggled at the thought of Molly's uptight parents wearing tie-dyed shirts and beads. "We ought to go."

Something caught her eye. She pointed out her bedroom window. Molly slipped closer.

"Granger and the Claw? Something's seriously out of whack."

"They're coming here," Erin said.

Molly followed her downstairs to let them in. They weren't inside a full minute before Granger said, "Getting ready for a trip to Demon's Bluff, eh? Very cool."

"How'd you know about that?" Molly blurted. Erin's warning look came too late.

Claudia kept her berry-red smile thin. "We're thinking of going, too, that's all. Everybody who's anybody is heading there. Wondered if we could split gas costs, maybe help drive."

Erin wanted to laugh. The Claw was such a poor liar. But if it could help them in some way . . .

"Sure, but can we use your car, Claw?"

Claudia gave her silly hand signal and giggled. "Don't see why not."

THE ANGEL CALLED the Shining One shook his head. The people below let themselves be used as chess pieces. Why did they allow such manipulation when God gave them choices, free will?

Another angel, less experienced in these matters, looked into the Shining One's eyes. "It's happening again."

"They don't learn fast."

"Will Patrick make it out alive this time?"

"Only the Father knows."

21

TREVOR HELD HIS hands over his ears as his special extra-credit project whined questions at him.

"I don't know!" he roared.

"You don't have to get so upset," Demon Girl said, pouting. "My name's Hope by the way."

Trevor grumbled.

Demon Guy crossed his arms. "I thought you were supposed to teach us stuff. We're bored."

"Um, sorry, Barry." Working alone sounded good, especially now.

Then he had an idea. A field trip. That's what they all needed. Get out of the apartment, get some fresh air. And Trevor knew who would love to meet them.

AT BREAKFAST JARROD said, "I could see how upset you were, so after you went to bed I hit redial and left a message for Erin. Told her how you were doing. Also told her about the Fest."

"I should be mad," Patch said, "but I really appreciate that." Erin knew where he was. Would she care to try and find him? He could only hope. "You'll like her."

Patch wondered whether Erin still liked him. Or if she ever had.

22

THEY DIDN'T SUSPECT a thing." Claudia looped her arm through Granger's.

"Not those two," he said. "They'll lead us right to Patch."

She leaned closer. "They're in their own world, and I hope they never find the exit sign."

"Don't you think they're going to catch on, with all those posters announcing the reward?"

"By then it'll be too late." Claudia slipped her fingers into Granger's hand as the Straight Arrow Summer Camp van drove by and Nancy stared out the window at them. She was clearly stunned, mouth open, hand raised.

Granger didn't wave. *Good.* Claudia snuggled into his shoulder as Nancy struggled to keep them in view.

"Best part is that we never had to mention the creep by name."

HEY DON'T CARE about you. They care only about each other.

Nancy stuck fingers into her ears. Shouting at invisible voices wasn't winning her any sanity points. That's why she was on the road to the camp for troubled girls. *Troubled.* She hated that word. Tears fell.

The brochure said campers prepared meals, scrubbed toilets, and washed staff cars. Maid for the summer. *How much are my parents paying for this?* She could only imagine. At least she wasn't in chains, like at New Peace Clinic. No medicine for her this time. Only fresh air, flowers, and deer.

And best of all, you have me.

That perky tone. She wanted to tear it from her mind. To scream. Instead she held her breath and felt her face warm. This was all because of that ring. Her finger was red and swollen from trying to claw it off.

Claw. Wonder what she's up to?

Get out of my head! Nancy lost it, doubled over sobbing. "Please!"

Make me.

*HEY WON'T EVEN know." Cheryl McCry forced a smile. "Believe me. This will work."

"You have your ways," Trevor said, polite as ever. "I have mine."

McCry stood and leaned on the desk. "I want to continue working together, but I must see results."

"Me, too, Ms. McCry."

She walked him out to the waiting room where he introduced

two fellow teens as his cousins. Usually McCry felt ill at ease around children, but these two appeared harmless. Hope and Barry. Nice names. Their smiles seemed genuine and their teeth perfect. Like catalog models.

Since when do teenagers not have pimples? These two sure were lucky.

23

ERIN BRACED HERSELF in the backseat with Molly as Claudia's car swerved.

Keep your eyes on the road, Claudia, she thought.

"I will."

"Will what?" Erin said.

"Keep my eyes on the road."

Now the Claw could read her mind? Perfect.

It was six in the morning, and they expected to drive all day and arrive by dinner. Should be some adventure with the Claw at the wheel.

Hungry, Erin thought. *I'm ready for breakfast.*

"Don't worry," Granger said, craning his neck at her from the front passenger seat. "We'll stop when everyone gets hungry. You're not the only one on board."

Huh? What was she doing, thinking aloud? This was too weird.

Well, just in case, she forced from her mind Patch and the real reason she and Molly wanted to go to Demon's Bluff.

Y OU'RE IN A PRECARIOUS SPOT." Pastor Ron pointed a thin finger at Patch. "I want you to understand what you're up against."

Patch and Jarrod were meeting with the minister privately.

"Honestly," he said, "I don't worry much about the festival. My job is to keep my flock spiritually strong so they won't be affected by it. That seems like a solid biblical approach to me. All the hype is just that." He scratched the back of his hand. "As for the rest of the town, I'm not so sure."

Jarrod jumped in. "That's what we've been thinking. When we get involved, selling stuff to the visitors, it's like we're saying it's okay to come once a year and seek Satan."

The minister shrugged, and Patch could sense his mind whirring. "What are you suggesting? Giving up the profits and being more proactive about souls?"

"Yes," Patch said. "Hold rallies, prayer gatherings, let the tourists know that not everyone here likes the idea of connecting with the devil."

"Well, you know this town was built on the site of a great spiritual battle." The pastor rubbed his eyes. "Least that's what I've always heard."

"Then it's time both sides are represented again, don't you think?"

Jarrod leaned toward Pastor Ron. "You taught me to care for people I don't even like. Let's find a way to reach people we don't even know."

Pastor Ron studied the vaulted ceiling. "Guess we've gotten fat, not worrying about the World Peace Alliance. Pretending they're not out there. You know if we pursue this course, we'll bring them running."

"That's nothing new to me," Patch said.

"That could be the end of you," the pastor said. "But if you're willing, I sure can be too. I don't ever want to forget what God has done for us."

24

NANCY SLIPPED THE paperback into her pocket and watched the highway disappear as the van pulled onto a winding road and up a steeply curved path to the camp at the very top of the hill. Away from everything. Great.

She had to admit it was pretty. Breathtaking, actually.

What an incredible view.

She waited. Nothing. No mental noise, no response. She yanked. The ring still stuck tight, but at least she was not being tormented by the voice.

A thin woman welcomed her with a handshake, and Nancy felt the squeeze all the way up her arm. Miss Grady, her badge read, with a straight arrow beneath the letters.

"Hi. Some view."

Miss Grady nodded, obviously proud. "We were lucky this land was donated to the cause." She led Nancy to a row of rustic, narrow cabins marked by low roofs and mounted the steps of one of them. "This is where you'll be bunking. You and the other five."

"Six in this little shed?"

"No problem. There are two triple bunks."

Inside Nancy met five sets of suspicious eyes, conversations halting as though they'd fallen off a cliff. "Girls, meet Nancy."

Two benches sat in the center with the bunks pushed to the wall. Where were the mirrors? Showers? Sinks? Toilets?

"Where's the bathroom?" was all she could manage.

A girl on a bottom bunk stretched and let out a laugh. "You mean she doesn't know?" She was muscular and heavily made up. The others seemed to look at her with admiration. Nancy didn't like her harsh, mocking voice.

The group was staring again, and Nancy wished she'd kept her mouth shut.

"This is Lori Irons," Miss Grady said. "Here for her second summer."

Nobody would come here by choice, let alone twice.

Lori squeezed out of the bunk and pushed past her admirers. "The outhouses are six cabins away." She pulled Nancy outside, and the others followed like ants after sugar.

"Showers are over there." Bare legs showed below a log screen.

"Thanks, Lori," Miss Grady said. "I knew I could count on you to make our new camper feel welcome."

"Happy to help."

Nancy was beginning to feel very alone.

You haven't forgotten me already, have you?

She worried she might actually welcome the voice now. It was as close to familiar as she had, almost an old friend.

Nancy smiled at Lori and shook Miss Grady's hand again. "Thanks for the tour. I'm going to love it here."

She enjoyed the surprised looks. *They don't know who they're dealing with*, Nancy thought.

They certainly don't.

T HE ANGEL WITH long hair, the Radiant One, motioned to Nancy. "She's the one."

His companion, nearly a twin, shrugged. "God has his reasons."

"This girl is in deep trouble. Thinks she has the upper hand because she can access a voice in her mind."

"Doesn't she realize . . ."

"Of course not." The Radiant One crossed his arms and waited. "She's only human."

P ATCH SCANNED THE e-mail message and turned to Jarrod. "It's from Gary. Least I think it is. We don't use real names."

"Why hadn't he gotten back to you sooner?"

"Says he's sorry, wishes he could help, but that God's got other plans for the Tattooed Rats. They have to head underground for a while." Patch shook his head. "I never thought about what they might be going through. I've always worried about myself first. Some friend."

He typed back, "Praying for you too. No worries, no rush. It's in God's hands."

Man, when would he learn that he wasn't the only game in

town? Well, Tattooed Rats or not, Patch had his own things God had given him to do. He wouldn't be going anywhere for a while.

And that felt good.

Y OU SENSED IT too?"

"Oh, yeah," Molly said. She pulled Erin's arm. They stood near the garbage can several yards from the restrooms where Granger and Claudia had gone a few minutes before.

"They're reading our minds," Erin said. "Scares me to death."

"How?" Molly kept looking back. "What does it mean?" They only had seconds.

"I don't know, but whatever you do, try not to think about Patch. That's the only way to protect him."

"I'm trying. But you know how the more you try not to think about something, the more you do."

"Takes discipline, Molly. Prayer is the only answer."

Molly pulled Erin to the "Doggy Play area" where several pooches frolicked and barked. *The more distractions the better,* Erin thought. She kept her eyes open as Molly pleaded with God to help them control their thoughts and keep them from Claudia and Granger. Peace and hope washed over her like cool rain on a hot day.

Claudia and Granger approached.

"Cute dogs, huh?" Erin said.

Claudia formed a claw. "Loud and noisy. Can't hear my own thoughts."

25

"ITHER PAY ATTENTION or go home!" Trevor used his real other-worldly voice instead of the calm human tone that went with his costume.

Hope and Barry stared out their separate windows. Silent for the moment. "Sorry," they managed.

Trevor was back, along with his calm human voice. "Just don't let yourself get distracted."

"You scared us," Demon Girl said, frowning.

Demon Guy nodded. He seemed to be the thinker of the two.

"I meant to," Trevor said. "You must understand that we're in a battle. It's not a game. We will die unless we pull more souls into the kingdom. We either draw humans into the darkness or they will head elsewhere."

"The 'H' word?" Barry said. He shuddered.

Trevor nodded. "And once they're in heaven, they're lost to us forever."

JARROD'S MOM LOOKED up from the ledger. "It won't be easy. What your father and I sell during the Fest helps us get through the winter."

"That's okay, Ma," Jarrod said. "These clothes will last me awhile. Least I'm warm."

His mother tapped her pen on the paper and winked at Patch. "You boys are right. We shouldn't have any part in that stuff. We don't believe a word of it."

Just seeing Jarrod interact with his mother made Patch miss his family even more.

BUT IS IT what God wants?" The Shining One stood with his back to his friend. "Have they been praying about the rally?"

"Yes, I see a stream of words, the colors of a sunset, leading to the throne."

"Then we leave it to the Father. If this is what he wills, they'll know."

"And if it's not?"

The Shining One turned and smiled. "They'll find that out too. My hunch, though, is that they're on the right track."

ERIN AND MOLLY'S visit had made McCry's day. Though they had not cracked under interrogation and the search of their purses for

names and numbers turned up empty, something even more important had been accomplished.

She ran a finger along the video map on her laptop, following
the red spot moving east. Not many places worth stopping at. She
looked at the names of the tiny towns. Demon's Bluff, Nevada.
That sounded like a possibility. She was glad at least one of the
Global Positioning System devices she'd had planted was func-
tioning. One was better than none. Later she'd find out if it was
Molly or Erin unwittingly betraying their friend. Didn't matter to
her; all these teens were the same.

Demon's Bluff? Would they pass through, or was that their
destination? McCry's fingers danced over the keyboard. Interesting.
The Demon's Bluff Spirit Fest. Food, fun, crazy visions, creatures
filling the sky.

All nonsense. But not a bad place to hide.

If her targets stopped in Demon's Bluff, she would go for her
own purposes. Patrick Johnson had to be there. This time she would
hang onto him, put him in chains if necessary. Make him pay for
embarrassing her.

THE RING THAT had so tormented her now seemed Nancy's only
connection with her old world. How was she supposed to sleep in
a room that sounded like a barnyard? She never knew girls could
snore like that.

When the yellowish glow appeared in the small square windows, she knew she had somehow made it through the first night.
She rolled up on her side with the covers up to her neck. She held
the ring close, like a precious jewel, and the familiar tingle began.

Good morning, my friend. Such a friendly tone. *What would you like to know today?*

Brightness filled her as she and the voice communicated in silence. And to think that just the day before she had desperately wanted to be rid of it.

Loud-mouthed Lori had annoyed her all day. But Nancy wasn't going to take it any more.

What bothers her? What's she afraid of?

Discovering and making use of that secret became Nancy's purpose in life.

26

CLAUDIA SLAMMED THE door. "When will those two let up with the goody-goody thoughts? They're making me sick."

"Same here," Granger said. "If they think about one more itty-bitty puppy, I'm going to heave. Tuning in to them is like watch-ing a nature film."

"Too sweet to be true," Claudia said, twisting a fingernail into her cheek. "What happened to the pictures of Patch? The mean mentions of me? They're hiding something. No one could be that squeaky clean."

NOT EASY, IS it?" Erin said.

Molly squeezed her temples. "You kidding? Almost impossible."

Erin pointed to the sign in the window of a store on Main

Street. Patch's face, shadowed and scared, the underlined "Reward" in huge red letters. "Wonder if he'll try to run again."

"I would."

"Keeping your angel wings clean?" Granger said behind them, grinning. Claudia was there too.

Oh, no!

Erin knew her mind flared like a torch because of the poster. She immediately tried to remind herself of the roly-poly puppies.

Granger's look turned hard. "Stop with the games. We know what you're thinking. And we already know about the reward for your friend." He opened up another poster crammed in his pocket.

Claudia blew a bubble with her gum. "You can't fool us."

"Why pretend, then?" Erin said.

The Claw stepped forward until they were toe to toe. "For some reason that creep trusts you. I don't know why, especially after you betrayed him."

Erin fought to keep quiet. Claudia and Granger headed back for the car. "Don't want to miss a minute of the Spirit Fest. Time to set up camp."

The two left Erin and Molly behind, Claudia marching like a band member, knees popping to her waist.

"What's up with her?" Molly said.

Erin shook her head. "Never knew it would be so tough to keep thoughts from cluttering my head."

"Puppies and kitties, here I come," Molly said, tightening the band on her ponytail.

"I'm going with mountain peaks and ocean waves."

TREVOR WAS GETTING a headache. Despite his attempts at self-control he was roaring again—that deep, low monster growl that got the attention of Hope and Barry, who were flopped back on the beat-up chairs in the kitchenette in his motel room. He could hardly wait to get out of this dull town.

"Stop yelling. It doesn't do any good." Demon Girl flipped her blonde hair over her shoulder. Trevor liked her better as a devil, jowly and covered with scales. With her costume on, she almost looked pretty. At least a human would think so.

"Stop whining. We've got work to do." Enough was enough.

Demon Guy's human lip trembled. "We'll be good."

"Not possible," Trevor said, laughing. "You're demons!"

"Go over it again, please, Trevor." Demon Girl pretended to be flirting. Scary how fast she'd learned the ways of teen girls.

He ignored her. "Our goal is to get Patrick. Shut him up and keep him from running down the demon lifestyle. Scare him into silence." Trevor gulped down an apple, then an orange. "That's something humans don't get: we can't force anyone to do anything."

"We just suggest," Barry said. "Whisper in their ears." His voice sounded like the sighing wind.

"Exactly. We get Patch to doubt himself, doubt his friends, doubt anyone who cares about him. Then we've got him. He'll make a mistake, and we'll be waiting."

Hope sidled up to Trevor. "Will we get extra credit too? I want a good grade."

"Listen carefully and stay out of my way, and you'll get what you deserve. Time to get to Demon's Bluff."

27

ANGELS SOMETIMES HAVE to work on their attitudes. The Shining One was glad he had an assistant keeping him company as he watched over Patrick Johnson. It was good having someone to talk to.

The younger guardian paced. "Shouldn't we warn him? They're all against him. What would be wrong with helping?"

"Everything. We cannot take a single step outside of God's will and still be called his servants."

"But doesn't God want Patch protected?"

"Of course, but he also wants Patch to learn more about him. Sometimes education hurts."

But he felt the same sometimes. Why all the waiting? Why ever let evil get the upper hand?

The answer was clear as ice over a mountain stream: God gave everyone a choice. They could do his will or strike out on their own.

The Shining One had seen it for centuries: seek God or satisfy self.

Even angels had that choice. Lucifer had once been known as a morning star.

CHERYL MCCRY STARED at her boss in the passenger seat, knowing it would bug her.

"Keep your eyes on the road, McCry," Teresa Frazier said. Brown hair lightly curled; full, pink lips; pale skin—Ms. Frazier could have been in the movies.

McCry couldn't believe Frazier had insisted on riding along to Demon's Bluff. Being around the woman made her feel homely.

Well, McCry decided, *I am who I am*. But that was the problem. Even with consultants telling her how to dress, how to walk, how to talk, how to smile, McCry felt like an outsider.

Act calm, be calm.

She repeated the words to herself, built a rhythm in her mind. *Act calm, be calm. Deep breath, ease off on the gas. Act calm, be calm.*

"You requested a king-sized bed for my room." It wasn't a question. Ms. Frazier added lipstick as she squinted into the mirror on the sun visor.

"Taken care of."

"And my fresh flowers. You requested roses, didn't you? Plus apples, plums, and pears."

McCry clamped her teeth tight and forced a nod, afraid of what she might say.

THEY CAN'T TREAT me this way, Nancy thought while scrubbing a toilet in the outhouse.

Certainly not, came the voice.

And in unison: *We have to do something about it.*

Cool, but kind of scary.

Tell me again about Lori Iron's weak spot.

The smooth voice flowed. *Mice, rats, rodents, even rabbits. Terrified of all creatures small and furry. Hates bugs too.*

Nancy sat up on her haunches and threw the rag to the floor. What a stench! But this was her job. Keeping the bathroom clean for all.

Otherwise, bugs and crawly things might be attracted.

And that would be bad, really bad. Nancy smiled.

Great thinking, Nancy.

Can hardly wait to hear her scream. Nancy covered her mouth to keep from laughing out loud.

GOD," ERIN SAID, "protect us. Keep our thoughts on only things that are right. Keep us from giving away our friend. And protect us from Claudia and Granger."

Praying with Molly at a picnic table in the middle of a dusty, desert park was perfect. No one could sneak up on them.

"Yes, God," Molly said. "Give us the chance to talk to Patch before Granger and the Claw get to him."

28

IT'S ABOUT TIME," Hope said, hopping out of Trevor's car at Demon's Bluff. "You drive so slow. When I get my license . . ."

"Hush," Barry said, sneering at Trevor. "You'll make him mad, and then you know what happens." The two screeched, imitating his roar.

Even Trevor had to laugh. Once the Patch Project was complete, he'd be rid of these two forever. Then he'd be completely, totally alone. That sounded good.

He saw Claudia bouncing toward him with Granger at her side. "The day is looking better," she said. Then she saw Trevor's sidekicks. "I see you're still babysitting." She glared at the teens. They returned the stare.

Trevor wanted to make this quick. Snag some information, get out. He trusted Claudia as much as she trusted him.

Claudia unrolled a wanted poster. Trevor showed it to his

assistants. "Make like bloodhounds and track down this guy. You'll get extra credit you won't believe."

Demon Girl shot Trevor a look. "We're going to hold you to it." She gave Claudia a twisted grin and flicked her tongue.

The two took the poster and ran off.

"Patch won't recognize those two."

"They're scary," Claudia said.

Granger nodded.

Not as scary as you two.

"That wasn't nice."

"I know." Trevor had given them the gift and he could take it away. All or part of it. He was getting tired of responding to their every whim.

That would have to stop.

P ATCH COULDN'T BELIEVE how the Prayer Rally had come together. The main service would be held atop Demon's Bluff. Booths would offer games for kids, free snacks, soft drinks, and cotton candy.

The heat could scorch a cactus, so the free ice water should get the most takers. Patch hoped wanderers would accept New Testaments and gospel tracts too.

"Couldn't do anything like this back where I come from," he told Jarrod, who adjusted his ball cap.

"Good stuff," Jarrod said, testing the cotton candy. "We should get a great turnout. A lot of people still want to make a quick buck, and the crowds are huge."

"What was Pastor Ron saying about how it got started?" Patch said.

"Legend says a century ago this plateau was the site of a great battle between angels and demons." Jarrod crutched his way to a table beneath the tarp.

"What happened? Why the big fight?"

"The people vowed to build a community dedicated to God. The story is that Satan sent his minions to tempt the towns-people. People got busy, stopped praying, stopped worshipping. The church died. When the time came for the big battle, only the demons showed up." He patted the bill of his hat. "Sad, huh? In our museum you can see paintings of that day. It happened on these bluffs where the Spirit Fest used to be held."

"So what happened?" Patch said.

"Supposedly, huge demon faces appeared. Red eyes, hungry mouths."

"What did the people do?"

"They gave up," Jarrod said. "Ran. A few years later someone decided that a Spirit Fest might make the demons happy."

Patch shook his head. "The angels lost interest? How could that be?" Seemed impossible. "Anyone at the museum I can talk to about that legend?"

29

ANGELS DO AS they're ordered, but they still have questions. The Radiant One wondered what watching over this mean girl was all about. She couldn't be a Christian, the way she was acting.

Nancy didn't have the whole picture. The Radiant One knew that. Humans never do. She couldn't know Lori was angry with her father for dying. Lori covered her fury by pretending to be in charge. That succeeded in scaring people, but she also made enemies fast.

All the angel could do for now was watch.

GET MY LUGGAGE."

She had her own bags to carry, but McCry pushed the door wide with an extended foot for Ms. Frazier, who swayed through

like a model. Some motel. Looked more like a ski lodge. McCry's
blood pressure bubbled. Helping like some bellboy wasn't her style.

All she had to do was find the girl with the tracer in her purse
and follow her to the prize.

After getting herself and her boss checked in, McCry found
Frazier on a couch in the lobby flipping through a newspaper. She
stood. "Finally. I'm bored."

"I've narrowed the tracer to the exact campsite."

Not even a word of congratulations or thanks.

Someone appeared at her side. "Lost, young man?" And then
she recognized the short, spiky hair, and the toothy smile. She
should have known Trevor would be here.

"Ms. McCry, pretty as a poster," he said.

"Very funny."

"And this is?" Frazier said, extending her hand.

"Another informer," McCry said. "Not too trustworthy, though."

ONCE SHE SET her mind to it, she could accomplish anything. In
a few hours, Nancy had absconded with sugar, peanut butter,
raisins, jelly, crackers, and more—enough to attract a forest full of
vermin. She'd load up the space beneath Lori's bottom bunk with
goodies, hopefully tempting every mouse, rat, rabbit, and insect
within smelling distance. The darkness couldn't come soon enough.

Love it, the voice said. Always there, always comforting.

As the rest of the girls snored, Nancy plopped blobs of peanut
butter atop the mess, then laid a trail of snacks to the doorway and
tossed tidbits on the doorstep. She crawled into bed. Before she

could even close her eyes, a mass of creatures swarmed. Almost as though they'd gotten directions.

Sweet dreams.

HOW THE RADIANT One wished he could whisper in Nancy's ear about the hole in Lori's heart. But she wouldn't listen. She was set on having her own way.

Lori wouldn't be the only one to pay. That the Radiant One knew from centuries of experience.

30

ERIN ALMOST CHOKED on her gum as Claudia and Granger stole a row of cookies from a large platter. So what if it was dinner time? That was no way to act.

"They're free," a woman with long gray hair said. "No need to sneak." Her smile looked real. She offered some napkins.

Claudia refused them and clapped the crumbs from her fingers before throwing the extras snacks away. "So where are you two going?"

Erin didn't know what to say. They'd been searching without luck for Patch. She imagined Claudia already knew that.

Or did she?

"Well?" Claudia said, tapping her foot.

Erin was intrigued to find that her thoughts had apparently been shielded. *I'd enjoy rubbing those chocolate cookies in your shimmering blonde hair.* She kept her smile steady.

Still nothing.

"We were taking a walk, that's all."

"Better be all," Granger said. He pushed his sunglasses back on his head.

Erin didn't like the new Granger.

"They didn't know." Molly kept her voice low.

"You know why?"

Molly nodded. "Prayer. There's no other explanation."

"God kept us from blowing Patch's cover. Now let's find him." The two pushed through the crowds.

Erin didn't see him anywhere. But a yard away, a boy on crutches caught her eye. He flew along almost like he didn't need them. His name tag read JARROD.

Erin motioned Molly to follow. "Jarrod!" Erin shouted. The boy turned, clearly confused. "I'm Erin. I'm looking for Patch."

"I talked to you on the phone," he said, smiling. "C'mon."

FAMILIAR FACES," THE Shining One said. "Trevor knows we're here."

"He acts like he owns Demon's Bluff," his assistant said.

"Technically he does." The Shining One paced. "The humans handed it over years ago."

"Why don't we take it back?"

The Shining One felt the same but pushed the urge away.

"God gives people choices."

"And they usually make the wrong ones."

"Sometimes they learn." The Shining One pointed to the huddle of teens below. "At least we can hope."

PATCH COULDN'T BELIEVE it. They'd come for him. He embraced Erin and Molly and asked about Nancy. Their silence told him a great deal. Erin finally said, "She's not the same; neither is Granger."

"What about you-know-who?" Patch said, curling his fingers like a claw.

"The same," Molly said.

Jarrod had not wanted to intrude, but now he said, "If the unbelievers are your friends, why don't you just talk to them about Jesus, come out and say what you're thinking, tell them why you're worried?"

Erin leaned back on her heels. "In a perfect world, maybe."

"They need the truth," Jarrod said, tapping the tip of his crutch.

"I appreciate what you're saying," Patch said, "but it's not that easy. You think I could just talk to anyone I like with all those posters around?"

Jarrod shrugged. "Someday, I hope. May truth reign once and forever."

"Terry asked me to give you this, Patch," Erin said, wrapping her arms around his neck.

Patch couldn't help but smile. "Hey, thank him for me. And give this one back to him from me."

Erin touched her fingers to her lips. "Sure, but I hope you can give it to him yourself."

Patch felt awkward but wonderful.

Molly yanked him out of the moment. "So what can we do to help?"

"Tomorrow the hordes arrive for the Spirit Fest," Patch said, explaining the history as he knew it. "It doesn't make sense that angels actually gave up the town. That's not how God works. We're on our way to the museum to see if we can learn more."

31

So what's the news?" Claudia asked. She was tired of waiting and ready for action.

"Happy to see you too," Trevor said.

"Whatever. Your clueless posse still out searching? Why don't we all look for Patch?"

"Fine," Trevor tromped off. "You go your way and keep out of mine," he said as he rounded a booth.

"What's the idea, Claw?" Granger said. "You don't trust him, and neither do I."

"'Course not. But if you follow him, we'll know if he knows where Patch is. C'mon, Grange, don't look like that. Think about the prize." *Of course, if I find Patch first, I won't have to share.*

She looked up quickly. But if he'd heard her thought, Granger must have decided she was joking. Yeah, of course she was.

His face showed frustration. He was trying to figure something out. "You know, sometimes I'm not sure we've chosen the right side." He fiddled with his ring.

"Maybe not," Claudia said. "But the fringe benefits are amazing." She polished her necklace. "I'll let you in on a secret, Grange. You can turn off the little annoying voice if you want. I figured out how."

He looked doubtful. "I don't think we can control these things." He pulled on the ring. It stuck tight. "See?"

"Sure we can. If you're tired of getting unwanted advice, just keep using it to pick up thought waves of friends, enemies, and strangers. It keeps the voice quiet." Claudia widened her stance. "Trevor was right. We *can* control the darkness. If we're not afraid."

Granger didn't look convinced. "If you believe the word of a demon." He pulled again at the ring. She saw his red finger.

"All you have to do is ask it to stop. Simple as that."

Granger ignored her, intent on extracting his finger from the ring.

Whatever. Let him mope. Claudia would use the power whenever and however she wanted. She was free of Trevor's know-it-all tone. It felt good being in charge of her life for once.

MOLLY STARED AS crowds began to arrive by the busload. People poured into the streets, more than enough to pack both the festival and the prayer rally.

Patch and Erin sharing that long hug had changed Molly's mind about going along with them to the museum. Not that long ago *she'd* been Patch's closest friend. They'd talked about everything, and she'd believed he cared. Maybe he had only been worried about her soul.

Molly felt like a leaky boat in white water.

A large sign listed all the activities for the Spirit Fest. Lots to do. Concert tonight. Big-name band. And it was free.

Time in the enemy camp might give her some ideas. What did she have to be afraid of? She had talked to God and he'd answered. All she had to do was call his name, and he'd come to her rescue. *Pray and he'll answer. No big deal.*

She ran her finger down the printout tacked to the bulletin board. Fifteen minutes until the next show—comedy/magic. Might be fun. Better than a museum.

But as she tried to blend in with the crowd, a strong hand clamped onto her shoulder.

"Molly." Cheryl McCry smiled broadly. "Good seeing you again."

"What are you doing here?" Molly felt trapped.

"Probably the same thing you are. Looking for someone. So, is Patrick here?"

"I couldn't tell you," Molly said, forcing herself to calm down. That wasn't exactly a lie. Maybe she should pray, but McCry scared her.

A pretty woman at McCry's elbow punched keys on an electronic device no bigger than a wallet.

"Remember," McCry said, "you run into Patrick Johnson, you let me know."

Molly nodded and hurried away. She'd hardly taken ten steps when Claudia accosted her. "You're such a fool."

Great, another of my least favorite people.

"That's not a nice thing to think," the Claw said. "So, what did McCry want?"

"I'm sure you know," Molly said. Why couldn't she bring herself to stop and pray? Claudia was obviously tuned back into her thoughts, so she might as well put it all on the table.

"You're the reason she's here," Claudia said.

Molly wrinkled her brow. "Me? No way."

"Give me your purse."

"No!"

Claudia yanked it from her and dumped everything in the dirt. Molly grabbed up her license and wallet.

Claudia turned the bag inside out, feeling along the bottom.

What is this crazy girl doing?

"Crazy, huh?" Claudia tore open a seam and produced a tiny circuit board. "A tracking device. A little bird told me that it was planted by your special friend."

McCry tracked us? She must have bugged our purses when we were questioned. Some answer to prayer. "God, help me," she said. But did she mean it?

Wait. Molly had to focus on the One who gave her strength, the One who Patch and Erin believed in. She thanked God for protecting Patch, for pulling her away from him and the others. God had used her lousy loner attitude to rescue Patch, at least for now. And he'd used the Claw to reveal how deep was the danger called McCry.

Nancy hardly slept all night, listening, waiting. She muffled a giggle when Lori roused and said, "I've got to use the facilities."

Go ahead. Go right ahead.

Good one, the voice said.

Lori swung her feet off her bunk, and Nancy rolled up on an elbow with a ringside seat for the fright of the century. The shrieking began. A stuck siren.

The others immediately awakened. Some rushed to Lori, trying to shoo away the beasts. But they wouldn't budge. Lori bellowed.

"What a chicken!" Nancy said. "Bawk! Bawk!" She leaped from her bed, stuck her thumbs under her arms and flapped her wings. Others joined in.

Lori stopped squawking and burst into tears.

"What a baby!" Nancy said.

But now the other girls stopped laughing and began glaring at her. Apparently it had stopped being funny.

"Lori, you okay?" someone said, reaching for her. Lori buried her face in her pillow.

Nancy crawled back into bed and faced the wall. She had given Lori what she deserved, so why the sick stomach?

She got what she deserved, the voice said. *You're a hero.*

Nancy wanted to scream, but it wouldn't do any good.

She knew the voice was wrong.

32

THE RADIANT ONE chuckled when he saw Nancy on her knees with her sudsy buckets and rags, a pale, pathetic Cinderella. She worked alone on the mess while the others ate sweet rolls for breakfast.

But he also felt sorry for her, knowing that wicked forces had influenced her. Her ring was a clue. It sparkled as Nancy lifted her hand from the water. A bird, talons outstretched. That meant . . .

Trevor. Another of his tricks.

Nancy was helpless to remove the ring unless she sought assistance from God. Humans didn't understand how often they needed help from above. They couldn't just snap their fingers and make everything all right.

Such magic thinking happened only in fairy tales.

If only she would pray, though, maybe the Radiant One would be assigned to pluck the ring from her swollen finger.

Patch wondered what was up. Molly was back, bubbly, excited. Something had happened to her. Her ponytail danced as she spoke.

"From now on, we stick together," she said, spilling everything about seeing McCry and understanding for the first time how God truly protected her. "Prayer counts. Prayer matters. I see that now."

Patch pulled her to the enormous mural painted across the two-story wall at the back of the museum. "You've got to see this."

The scene showed Demon's Bluff with its flat tabletop and wind-carved rocks. Dust swirled, and at the far right hovered a mass of white clouds. An enormous demon face floated in front—fanged, reptilian, shiny red. The eyes were huge shimmering globes, the brow furrowed. The demon was not alone.

Jarrod and Erin sat taking in the enormous picture. "Look at them. Rows and rows."

"An army of evil," the old curator said, hobbling up. "My great-grandfather was there."

"But where were the angels?" Patch said. "Where was God?"

"That's always the question," the old man said, pointing into the drooping, glazed eye of the largest demon. "Whenever something bad happens, God gets the blame."

"I didn't mean—"

"Sure you did. We all do. We think of God as a big cuddly security blanket. We ignore him till we need him, then we wonder where he went."

He pointed to the town church with a tall white spire. "Look in the windows. Not a soul. Not in the streets either, see? Everyone fled. The so-called religious people feared Satan more than they trusted God."

"But what about the angels giving up on the town?" Patch said.

The man shook his head. "That's not what happened." He pointed to a mass of curling, thick clouds. "Those are the angels heading out of town. But it's not what you think. They were standing by, ready to rush in, but they never got the command."

"Because the people stopped praying," Patch said slowly.

HOPE SHOVED THE poster into Trevor's hands, her fingers sticky and purple from the cotton candy.

"Sorry," she said. "Couldn't find him."

"Yeah? How hard did you look? You didn't have any trouble finding snacks." Trevor wished again to be rid of these two. "You blew it."

Demon Girl stuck a hand on her hip. "You're in charge, Trev. You should be the one finding Patch. Not us." Barry the Demon Guy nodded and blew a bubble.

Trevor dragged the two behind an old warehouse. "Enough!" he roared, tearing his own mask off and shedding the rest of his costume. He slammed the two against a dumpster.

"Calm down, Trevor!" Hope whined. "We're sorry!"

Good. She was finally, fully fearful. "I am too," Trevor said.

Maybe this was just another test to see what he would do with incorrigible students. Trevor no longer cared. With one annoyance in each curled claw, he lifted them over his head. Then he tipped back his enormous mouth and snapped his teeth.

"Don't eat us!" Barry bellowed.

Trevor laughed and tossed them into the dumpster, where they rattled against the sides.

He peeked in at the two cowering under newspapers and heaps of rotted food. "Be gone!" he growled, closing his eyes.

If this didn't work, he might have to eat them after all.

He opened his eyes and reached in, stirring the stinking stuff. Gone. No sign of them. *Hmm. Never know what you can do until you try.*

33

NANCY DIDN'T WANT to miss out on the field trip to the Demon's Bluff Spirit Fest the next day.

"You shouldn't be allowed after what you did to Lori," Miss Grady said. "What were you thinking?" She squeezed her mouth into a knot.

Nancy hadn't been thinking, of course. She had been listening. Listening to the cursed voice in her head. She had gone from hating it to loving it and now hating it again. It only got her in trouble.

You smiled when Lori cried, remember. You're sick.

Nancy pressed her hands over her ears.

"What's wrong?" Miss Grady said, looking alarmed.

Nancy let her hands drop. "I'm sorry."

Was she ever! Sorry she'd accepted the ring, sorry she'd been caught, most of all sorry she couldn't think without that gremlin harassing her. How could she get rid of the thing?

The woman put her arm around Nancy. "We all make mistakes."

Nancy knew what was expected. She'd seen it before, done it before. "Oh, thank you, Miss Grady. Please give me another chance. I want to be Lori's friend."

Miss Grady grinned. "I love happy endings," she said, squeezing Nancy's shoulder.

Who knows? Nancy thought. *Maybe things will work out for me.*

Why should they? You, of all people, don't deserve a sweet ending. You're mean.

Shut up! Shut up! Shut up!

Poor Nancy. The Radiant One wasn't about to let her attend the Fest without him. He'd stay close, even if she had no idea he was around. God wanted his angels around even if people didn't know or care.

An angel's life wasn't his own. He did the will of the Maker and from that came great joy. And sometimes much sorrow.

Maybe someday Nancy would choose to serve the Savior, understand the meaning of true peace. Until then, the Radiant One would keep watch, wondering about these strange creatures called humans.

Prayer is the key," Patch said.

Erin, Jarrod, and Molly sat with him around a small table in the church library.

"That's what you've been saying all along," Jarrod said.

"I know," Patch said. "But that was when I saw prayer as a sort of magical way to fulfill wishes. Not any more. I even saw the prayer rally as an alternative to the Spirit Fest. Now I see it as important on its own, a chance to seek God."

Molly popped her chair legs down. "That meeting with McCry made me realize God was guiding me."

"I think we've finally got a God's-eye view," Patch said. "That cloud of angels in the museum mural is as real as we are. I think they're still around, waiting. At the right moment during the rally we need to forget the games, forget the free food, leave the booths, and walk away."

"Huh?" Molly didn't get it.

Erin, her brown-green eyes sparkling, seemed to understand. "And they'll follow us to where the others are seeking the spirit of Satan."

"Exactly," Patch said. "Wouldn't it be cool to call heaven down on them?"

34

PATRICK AND THE others finally saw prayer accurately, which made the Shining One burst into a hymn to the King.

His assistant beamed, shining with anticipation. "It's going to happen soon, isn't it?"

"At exactly the right moment," the Shining One said. "We will be released to do what we could have done generations ago." He breathed deep. "At least I think so."

NANCY LOOKED UP from her barbecued turkey drumstick. Oh, great. Second to Lori, he was probably the last person she wanted to see.

"Granger." She wiped her mouth. "What are you doing here?"

"Claudia and I—"

Nancy got the picture all at once. She should have known.

"Of course, the two of you. She's perfect for you, Grange." She stuffed her mouth so she wouldn't have to talk to this jerk.

"That's not it."

She rose to leave, but Granger kept cutting off her escape route. He seemed to be trying to get her to look him in the eye. *He must want me to spit this in his face.*

"No," he said. "You don't have to do that."

"Huh?" *Wish I had something to drink.*

"Here," he said, offering his soda.

"Thanks." She didn't mind if she did. "You're what?"

"Hm?" Granger said. "I didn't say anything." He smiled that slow smile of his, the one she liked.

"I thought I heard you apologize."

Granger took Nancy's hand. "You did." He showed her his ring. "I've got one too. We can read each other's minds. And have demons chew us out."

I'm so tired of this, she thought.

"Me too," he said, giving his ring a yank.

"I want to get rid of mine," she said, tearing up. "But it's impossible. I even tried butter."

"Me too." Granger made a show of pulling on his ring some more.

"That looks painful," Nancy said.

"It is. But not as bad as feeling like something else is controlling me." Granger sat at a bench and made room for Nancy. "I've been worried about you. Claudia said we can control how much information we get from these things." He twirled his ring. "We just have to think hard."

"I'm sure the Claw has been real concerned about *us*," she said.

"You aren't listening. Maybe we can still listen in without getting pushed around by the voice in our heads."

"That would be nice," Nancy said. "A relief, in fact." She thought about what happened at the camp, how she felt prodded, forced to do things she didn't want to do.

Granger looked at her with big, sad eyes. Perhaps he did understand. He was slouched, long legs crossed at the ankles. He was a nice guy, and she'd forgotten how much she liked him.

"Weren't you trying to make me jealous?"

"No, I was trying to talk to you. Every time I got close, Claudia was in the way, her big nose in my business."

"You've never been interested in Claudia?"

"No." Granger looked away. "Okay, for a while I thought she was all right. But you and I both know this ring wasn't much of a gift. Not with someone always trying to get into our heads."

Nancy looked at her watch. "I've got to go. I was supposed to meet my group for dinner. Miss Grady will kill me if I'm late."

Granger looked sad, and Nancy knew it was because she was leaving. She had heard his thoughts. It was no act. He cared about her.

W HY DO THEY *always forget what God has done for them?*

The Radiant One wished Nancy had told Granger about the night weeks before when she'd prayed for his life, when Granger's doctors thought he was going to die.

Did Nancy even remember? Whenever something forced her to think or even seemed inconvenient, she'd push it from her mind.

Think, girl, think.

So you agree?" Patch said, excited.

"Of course," Pastor Ron said. "I'll get in touch with other church leaders and make sure we're all on the same page."

Patch was surprised that Erin kept still. He could see she was working up to saying something. "I don't want it to be a show," she said finally, flushing.

"C'mon, Erin. You know me better than that."

"Maybe. It's just that I thought there was a verse about going to a quiet place to pray. We're not supposed to parade our prayer before people."

"The point is," Pastor Ron said, "God looks at our hearts. If this is done with the right motive, God will bless it."

Patch was glad to see Erin smiling again.

35

THERE WAS NO point denying it, Trevor decided. He was incredible. He could do anything he wanted. Even make irritating tagalongs disappear with the power of his voice.

He admired himself in the hotel room mirror. He was huge, with blood-red biceps and bulging thighs. Impressive. But it was time to get back in disguise. He yanked the fake skin over his limbs and slipped his powerful body into the weak human state others so admired.

He couldn't believe how easy it had been to rid himself of those two whining annoyances. Maybe he could do more. The sky was the limit when you were developing demon skills.

Not an hour before, Trevor had dreaded even the thought of another day in this dull, dusty town. Now he could hardly wait for the Spirit Fest to begin.

O<small>N</small> S<small>ATURDAY</small> <small>NIGHT</small> Patch would be part of the First Annual
Demon's Bluff Prayer Rally. As people passed during the day, he
handed out flyers and offered to pray with anyone who desired it.
The occasional rebuffs didn't bother him.

Erin, Molly, and Jarrod went from booth to booth promoting
the event.

Patch saw a girl with tattoos on both arms, reminding him of
the small fish-shaped mark on his own ankle. He knew he should
include the Tattooed Rats in his prayers. Surely they were doing
the same for him.

At eight thirty in the evening the believers would move toward
the prayer circle campfire on Demon's Bluff. Patch couldn't wait.
He craved God's touch.

Suddenly he felt an icy cold crawl up his neck, despite temper-
atures in the 100s. What had caused that? Maybe all the posters he
kept ripping down all over the place. The last thing he needed was
some stranger recognizing him and dialing the reward hotline.

And then he saw him: Trevor, blond and trim, carried an armload of posters and was slapping them on every telephone pole
and blank wall and window he came across.

Patch slipped behind a large booth and knelt in the rock-strewn
aisle. He didn't worry who might see him or what they might say.

He prayed.

And when he opened his eyes, Trevor stood over him, already
on his cell phone.

"Didn't know cowards showed their faces in the daylight."
Patch stood and yanked Trevor's spiky hair. Obviously he didn't

feel a thing. The guy didn't make a sound or even blink. Patch realized for the first time that Trevor's eyelashes were stuck on over the holes to allow the thing hiding beneath to peek out.

Trevor whacked Patch's hands away. "People will wonder."

"Great idea! Hey folks, gather 'round. See the frightening son of the devil."

"Would you shut up?" Trevor backed away, scuffing up the red dust. People gathered, staring.

"Ashamed of your family?" Patch said. "Only like fighting in the dark?"

Trevor turned and ran, feet slapping the ground like horse hooves. He would be back, and Patch would be ready.

WELL, IF IT isn't Nancy, the wandering maid," Lori said. "So glad you could join us."

"Forgot about the time. Sorry, Lori. Sorry I'm late, sorry about everything."

Lori waved her off and turned back to her friends.

Miss Grady guided Nancy to the food line. "Thanks. I can tell you're trying to turn over a new leaf."

It was nice that she noticed, but what Nancy really wanted was to be rid of the cursed ring. She didn't want any portion of the thing's perverse power. She wanted to be rid of it completely: voice and all.

36

TREVOR BERATED HIMSELF for backing off when he could have torn Patrick Johnson to pieces. Hey, he was all-powerful, amazing. He'd been taken by surprise, that's all. What he needed just then was someone to admire him.

Someone like the Claw.

With this flood of people that might be a problem, except for the necklace he had given her. She hadn't seen everything the ring could do. Trevor stretched out his hand and turned in a circle, ignoring the wandering visitors who dodged him and looked at him like he was crazy.

Trevor pointed down the street and sensed Claudia's fear. He couldn't see her face yet, but she was coming nearer, forced by his strength.

It was as though the great crowds of confused seekers gave him more power, fed his strength, and made him even more than he thought he was.

And he thought a lot of himself.

CLAUDIA WAS SURE she'd caught a glimpse of Patch and had been heading for him. But she was suddenly drawn another direction, somewhere she didn't want to go. Before she could catch her breath she was running, panting. She flew past people as if they were moving in slow motion.

What was happening?

Then Trevor stood before her, arm out, hand open. Suddenly she knew. He wanted her near, and she had no choice.

NANCY NEEDED TO think. Granger was her friend. He cared about her. Was he telling her the truth—that Claudia had gotten between them? That was her pattern: find information, hang people to twist in the breeze, pull them where they didn't want to go.

Nancy had seen it before, had even helped the Claw hurt others.

That's what bothered her. The things she found so disgusting in Claudia lurked in her own soul. Nancy also sinned often and enthusiastically.

She felt invaded, used, by the voice. Could Granger be right? Was there a way to free herself from its hold on her? There had to be another option. It seemed to flicker in her thoughts then fade.

She wiped her chin as she and the other girls ate. How could she get rid of the ring?

Impossible. You made the choice. Now you have to live with it. The laughter—the sick, low chortling—made Nancy cringe.

Maybe the voice was right. Why should she get another chance? She put her hands on her head and squeezed.

Something nagged at a cobweb-coated corner of her mind. A single word came to her, bright as a lighthouse.

Prayer.

Prayer can't help. It's too late. Prayer is for weaklings.

One thing about the voice: it always spoke when she was feeling weakest. Or when she was on the right track.

The memory flooded back—praying hand in hand with Patch and Erin for Granger. He was in the hospital, his father ready to pull the plug on the life-support machines. Everyone thought he had no chance.

But he did. And it started with their prayers.

Hers had been merely a plea for some evidence that God was real. When Granger recovered, she'd had her answer. But she pushed it aside. It didn't fit her life.

Nancy needed God, needed someone who cared about her, who wasn't out to use her or control her.

The voice screamed, *Stop it! You're a fool!*

So what if she was. Nancy stood and started walking. Everything stilled, quieted. Even the voice softened, slipped into a low grumble.

"God," she said, "I'm here. Do you still see me? Could you still love me?"

And there stood Cheryl McCry. *Oh, no. Why?*

Nancy wanted to run, to scream, to cry. She pleaded with God. *What about another happy ending?*

McCry clamped her arms over Nancy's. "Got some questions for you."

Prayer was a farce. And that horrid ring was still there.

But as McCry dragged her away, Nancy saw the ring split and fall to the ground.

God had answered her prayer. At least in part.

37

THE SHINING ONE wanted to cheer. Patch had stopped to pray, then gathered Jarrod, Erin, and Molly and told them what had happened with Trevor. Reason to hope, signs of growth. Patch had prayed instead of retreating from his personal demon. It was enough to make an angel sing.

I SHOULD HAVE known Trevor would show up," Erin said. "McCry's here, so it makes sense. They're both liars."

"And Christians never lie?" Molly said.

That was so like Molly, Patch decided. Had to dig, had to find out for herself.

"We all struggle," Patch said.

When Molly smiled the lines around her eyes crinkled. "I know."

McCry was here creeping around because Erin and Molly had

been tricked. That made Erin angry. She couldn't believe the woman would stoop to planting a tracking device. But then, why should she be surprised?

Molly and Erin clipped walkie-talkies to their belts.

"The only one I want keeping track of me is God," Erin said. "We can pretend to hide our thoughts, but to him they're as obvious as the freckles on your face."

"You're the one with the freckles," Molly said.

"You know what I mean. He sees us. Always. And that makes me feel good."

38

IT FIGURED THAT these creeps would find each other.

Still, Nancy was scared as Claudia tested the cords binding her arms and legs. "You should have stuck with us, and this never would have happened," Claudia said.

Nancy had never felt more alone, though the hotel room was crowded. McCry, Trevor, Claudia, and some woman named Frazier hovered nearby. "I've got to get back or they'll come looking for me," Nancy said.

"Miss Grady?" Claudia's eyes shone like black diamonds.

Nancy focused on McCry. "What have I done? You can't keep me here."

When Ms. Frazier took a breath to speak, Nancy was intrigued. She was one of the most beautiful women Nancy had ever seen. Seemed she would be sweet too.

Wrong.

"We own you," the woman said. "Your parents do what we tell them, and you do the same."

Frazier tightened the ties that bound Nancy and made her cry out. Silently she said, "God, help me."

Peace flowed through her. And best of all, no voice cut her down as she prayed.

Nancy was thankful to be free of the ring.

The pretty woman's face had contorted into a Halloween mask with witch's eyes and a howling mouth. She slapped Nancy.

"You need to lighten up, Ms. Frazier," Trevor said softly, but when he spoke, the stench of his presence gave Nancy a headache.

Frazier's head wagged. Her voice cracked, and she drew back for another swipe. Nancy saw Claudia cringe and McCry smile. But the slap never landed. Something stopped Frazier's hand. A tail—thick, strong, coiling.

Trevor had flung off his costume. Claudia cowered, hand over her mouth. Frazier fought like a trapped animal. McCry rushed to her boss's rescue, but too late.

The scent of dank woods was stronger now. Trevor's demon form brought Claudia to her knees, but Nancy was entranced. Terrified but unable to turn her head.

So it was all true. The demons she thought she had seen were real. Down deep she'd known it all along.

But why was Trevor helping her? What was he saving her from?

Or for?

McCry squirmed in one of Trevor's claws like a mouse caught by a giant cat. He held Frazier with the other. Trevor wrapped his tail around their legs. Nancy couldn't look away. He was enormous and growing, his thighs sturdy stumps, bulging with muscles encased in sparkling scales. The women thrashed, fighting to keep from being pulled closer to the open jaws.

Nancy saw Trevor's power expand. He was in control and didn't want anyone to forget it. Nancy made herself as small as possible. Maybe the monster would ignore her when he'd had his fill of this game.

Claudia crept to the door, but Trevor whispered, "Enough." She fell in a heap, arms covering her head.

Nancy prayed as never before. And she was not afraid.

THE RADIANT ONE prayed. "Please free me, Father. Let me run to her and scatter the enemies." He watched Nancy cower as Trevor roared in his pathetic bid for power. How many times had he observed this tired cycle?

Demons lose in the end. But until then they made life horrible for humans.

He wanted to help Nancy. Now.

"Soon." That was the message.

He felt peace. He could wait. And at the moment of God's choosing, he would obey.

PATCH SAT WITH Jarrod at the towering overlook, Demon's Bluff, as the sun descended like a tired fire. "Another hour and the prayers begin."

"I've already started," Jarrod said, crutches next to him as always.

Patch hesitated. Then, "Ever pray for, you know, healing?"

Jarrod shrugged. "Sure. But I've stopped. Maybe someday it'll happen. But for now God has said no. I don't know why."

"But you're okay with it?"

Jarrod leaned back. "I'm okay with him knowing what I need and what I don't." He traced the rim of his cap.

Patch felt humbled by such faith.

Jarrod struggled to his feet and Patch followed him to the fire ring. They had work to do before the crowds came.

39

TREVOR LIKED KNOWING he could crush these weaklings without breaking a sweat. But he had a better idea.

Nancy's eyes were closed, but her mouth was moving. The piddly creature thought she could accomplish something by praying.

He'd sent those two teen dropouts back to their own realm—to the place at the mouth of hell's abyss, the place where demons danced.

He could do the same with McCry and Frazier. He squeezed tighter and purposed in his mind, "Back to your beds, back to your places. Be gone, wicked ones, and leave no traces."

Only their perfume remained, like a bad-smelling candle. Why hadn't he thought of this before?

Trevor carried his costume to the bathroom. From there he heard the door open and slam and someone running down the hallway, then down the stairs. Claudia. Selfish and proud of it.

Of course, she'd thought nothing of Nancy. Left her bound, a victim of fate.

That's why he liked Claudia. They were so much alike.

Trevor barely fit in the bathroom, his demon form expanding, larger, stronger, harder to contain. He pulled the mask back on and squeezed into the costume, a coiled spring. He posed before the mirror like a bodybuilder. "Master," he said, "give me more of you. Make me more like you. Let me shake this town to its roots."

Trevor returned to the room, to Nancy.

WHEN TREVOR PRODUCED the knife, Nancy thought she would die. But he cut the ropes, untwined her cords.

Why would he set her free? An answer to prayer? That's all she could think. A strange, bizarre, unexpected reply. But it made no sense.

Trevor had to have a reason. Nancy wouldn't worry about it now. She fled, tearing down the hallway. She expected Trevor to leap upon her at any moment.

Instead Trevor waved from the window, watching. Nancy had to find Granger, warn him. He would know what to do. He was that kind of a guy. She had to find Granger before Claudia did. And certainly before Trevor did.

But where was Granger in this huge throng? Words and laughter mixed like stew.

There! Dark hair, thin face. Nancy shouted and waved, but she could hardly hear herself. He glanced her way, brow knit, and moved on.

The ring was gone, the band around Nancy's heart snapped. She could breathe again, think again. No more excuses.

She would do the right thing.

P*RAY. DON'T STOP praying.*

The Radiant One watched and soon it was clear: Nancy was praying like Jonah on a stormy night. Once the sky cleared, the prayers stopped.

"No one but God can save you," the Radiant One wanted to shout. "Not Granger. No one." He looked heavenward, but Nancy was not yet ready for intervention. She still had to learn what trust truly meant.

40

PATCH WAS SEARCHING for kindling with Jarrod when he found a mound of sticks, a crisscross cave of twigs.

"Better leave that alone," Jarrod said.

"Why? It's perfect." Patch yanked at a small branch, making the entire structure shake. "We can use the whole thing."

"Some pack rat built this for its family."

"We need it more than he does."

"Those rats bite," Jarrod said.

"You're scared of a little—" Patch leaped back at a hiss. "Wow! It's big as a cat!" He prodded it with a stick.

The animal's eyes were glassy, its teeth bared, mouth wet with drool. "Guess we should look somewhere else," Patch said, but he slipped in the gravel and the rat was on him. Teeth dug into his leg and held on.

Jarrod whacked the animal with a crutch until it scurried off. The bloody marks on Patch's calf burned.

"We've got to get that cleaned," Jarrod said, leading Patch away from the circle and past streams of people.

"I've got to be back for this," Patch said. He couldn't stand the idea that he might miss the whole thing just because he'd wanted a bigger, better bonfire.

CLAUDIA GRABBED EVERY guy who looked remotely like Granger and spun him around. As soon as she found him she would get to her car and leave town. Forget Erin and Molly. Forget Patch. She didn't want to be around when Trevor figured out what to do with all his power.

Claudia knew it was callous to leave Nancy alone with the beast, but she had her own skin to save.

Suddenly Granger stood before her, his face in hers. "Where is she?" She saw something new in his face. Hurt? Concern? She wasn't sure.

"Who?"

"You know who! Nancy." The gaze of his light brown eyes flitted over her shoulder.

"No clue."

"I've got to find her. She could be in danger."

Claudia grabbed the necklace and felt the familiar warmth, but Granger's thoughts weren't coming through. She caught his hand.

The ring was gone.

"What makes you think she's in trouble?"

Granger walked away, calling over his shoulder, "I've been praying."

She didn't expect that. Claudia recoiled. Praying? The very word was an anvil on her chest. He was so smug. The fool. *If prayer does so much good, why is Trevor on the loose?*

Claudia still had her necklace, could still eavesdrop on weak, unprotected minds.

All she had to do was find one. Someone who wasn't dabbling with prayer.

P EOPLE MASSED AROUND the town square, packed together like logs in a pile. The courthouse was lit like day, a dramatic back-drop. The crowd swayed to thumping music. Every now and then Trevor heard a happy scream.

This was his kind of place. Young women smiled and nodded as he passed. Perfect. Ideal for a feeding frenzy.

Trevor would need help. He concentrated and sent a message to a couple of associates, explaining everything, telling them of the crowd, the dancing, the laughter. Like one insect telling another about a pollen source.

He felt the back of his teeth with his tongue. Best of all, these sheep seemed willing to listen to anyone. Anything.

This was going to be good.

41

PATCH SAT IN the church kitchen while Jarrod smeared antibiotic cream on his bite and wrapped his leg.

"Before we head back," Patch said, "let's stop in on the Spirit Fest and invite people to the prayer rally."

"I'm game if you are," Jarrod said.

"Can't think of anyone needing prayer more than all those demon chasers." Patch winced. He could do this if God helped him stand.

DON'T YOU SEE, Nancy?" Granger said. "God answered my prayer. How else could we have ever found each other in this crowd?"

"It's gone," she said. Nancy covered his ringless hand with her own and leaned close. "God, I'm asking you to prove yourself to me." Granger pulled back, but she wouldn't let go. "Get us out of here—now, safely."

"Stop, Nancy," Granger said. "That's not prayer. That's a test. You're asking God to do what you say, or else."

Nancy pushed back her hair. Granger could be such an idiot.

"So why pray?" she said.

"Maybe to determine what God has in mind, not tell him." Granger took her hand. "Let's try again."

Soon they were near the concert, the beat drawing them.

"I don't believe it," Granger said, pointing to the stage. "This I've gotta see."

"Trevor," Nancy said. He was acknowledging the applause of the crowd. She wanted to run, but with Granger protecting her, she followed him.

CLAUDIA WAS GOING the wrong way. People surrounding her kept pushing, pointing. Some sang. A fire snapped, swirled at the center.

I'm surrounded by crazies.

You got that right. The voice. It was back. Guess she didn't mind. She was feeling lonely. That's probably why it had returned.

Why did all these people look so happy, so excited? She was the one with the gift.

Some were like her, going toward the concert. But most looked like they were headed to the prayer gathering. Wouldn't hurt to let herself be pulled along toward the fire. Just to check things out.

Around the bonfire no one had chairs. Most had blankets and pillows. Without either, this was going to be uncomfortable and no fun. Why in the world was she here? These were weirdos, crazies, religious types.

Get out of here. Get out now. That nagging, whining voice. That's enough. She was sick of it. Claudia ripped the necklace off and the voice stopped.

Enough already. Let me hear. Let me think.

42

REVOR SUCKED IN the energy, the rush. He loved being on stage, and whatever he saw, he took.

The music made him bounce. Now he wanted the microphone, had to have it. Trevor didn't have to ask. All he had to do was look into the lead singer's eyes, and the man knew what to do. What he must do.

The music shuddered to a stop and the spotlights swung toward Trevor. "Thanks, man. Killer night in store for you." The crowd cheered. "But we're not the only show in town."

Loud boos rose from the crowd, but Trevor quieted them with a wave. "They have the right to gather, even if they're nuts. But what do you say we call down the sky on those clowns?" Trevor pointed toward the glowing fire atop the bluff at the edge of town. The people stood and screamed and waved.

"Let's ask our master to send rain that'll soak them to the skin!"

Cries and laughter rolled like a bulging wave and crested at Trevor's feet until he was certain he could walk on air.

P ATCH RAN TO the stage, forcing his way through people to reach Trevor. "May I speak? Or are you afraid of an opposing view?"

Trevor pursed his lips and squinted as people shoved Patch up onto the platform. Trevor tossed him the microphone, hatred in his eyes.

The glare of the lights blinded Patch, and when he spoke his voice cracked. He feared he sounded foolish, small.

"There is only one Master! And he is God, the Maker of the universe, the Ruler of all." Patch pointed at Trevor. "He's lying to you, urging you to worship evil. His master is Satan."

People jeered and threw cans, shoes, and food. Most missed, but some winged Patch on the shoulder and head. "There is only one true God. All else is an illusion, a lie."

Patch set the mike at his feet and strode off. The booing continued until Trevor smiled and said, "Ooh! Scary, huh?" Laughter rattled the stage and shook Patch's bones. "I challenge your puny god!" Trevor said. "Let's each ask for intervention and see where the real power lies. Call on your king, and we'll call on ours. Let's see who answers."

N ANCY HELD GRANGER'S hand, trembling. Things were getting too big too fast. She didn't like the look in his eye.

"I'm out of here," he said.

Nancy trailed him as he caught up with Patch and Jarrod. He reached back and looped his arm around her waist, and she felt stronger.

"Wait up, Patch!" Granger shouted. "We're with you, man."

43

PATCH'S WALKIE-TALKIE kept chirping. Molly, Erin. He forgot he'd promised to stay in touch. This was too important. He clicked off his receiver. Later, when things calmed down, he'd explain. They'd understand.

He and Jarrod and Granger and Nancy paired off on either side of the sidewalk. As people wandered by, one of the four would say, "Pray to the one true God."

Many looked down and hurried past. Some shouted profanities. Others said, "Shut up" or "Outta my way."

A few said, "Thanks. Maybe I will." Even fewer turned and headed for the prayer rally.

After nearly an hour they headed back to their own event. "Leg doing okay?" Jarrod said.

Patch nodded. "Feels a little warm."

"It's the desert," Jarrod said. "It rarely cools down much even at night."

"What about the challenge?" Granger said. "Shouldn't we tell someone? Shouldn't the pastor know what Trevor said?"

Patch thought Granger seemed nervous.

"What's the point?" Jarrod said. "It's not a contest where God hears the loudest voices. We're going to a prayer rally, not a football game."

Maybe Jarrod was right. This wasn't a competition. It was a chance to truly trust.

C LAUDIA WASN'T SURE if she was crazy or if it was the people around her who had lost their minds.

All they had been doing for an hour was praying, talking to an invisible god. How did anyone know he was even there, and if he was, whether he was listening?

Claudia wanted to grab her necklace and bolt, but she couldn't. Groups gathered, prayed, broke apart, reformed. One moment an old man prayed in a creaky voice, the next a young girl was on her knees.

These people actually believe.

They looked so typical, plain. Some thick, some thin, some sour, some smiling—all types. They were people like her friends, her mom, her grandpa. And either they were all wrong—silly and emotional—or they were onto something.

A child nearby prayed quietly, her face shimmering in the firelight. How could someone so young know for sure? Maybe she was just being brainwashed.

And then it hit her. How was she any different?

She went along with whatever her teachers told her, whatever her friends said was cool. She pretended to think for herself, but the truth was she went with the flow.

Not that she'd been trying, but if she'd picked up one thing from that Pastor Ron while sitting in this clump of Christians it was that it was *her* decision whether or not to follow God. Not making a choice meant rejecting God. Least that's what he said.

Claudia didn't like the idea of siding with Trevor, McCry, or her cohort. But what about people she cared about? Her grandparents, her mom?

If these people were praying to a God who was real, then what would happen to those who said no? Like her family did. God wouldn't *force* them to spend eternity in his presence.

People chose heaven or hell. They either chose to serve God or to blow him off, pretending he didn't even exist.

She had to make a choice. That thought burned like a white-hot coal.

44

T REVOR ROARED AS the voices of his fans grew bolder, fueled by alcohol, pumped by rage. Their anger caused him to glow and grow, and that made his costume painfully tight. Did he dare strip down to his true essence? He wasn't some teenage rocker. He was a demon of power, of purpose. Should he let these people see who he really was?

Not until his associates were in place. The clouds became stained the color of dried blood. The fools dancing at his feet were caught up in their chants and wouldn't notice. And if they did, they wouldn't care.

Trevor was about to offer Demon's Bluff to his master. But this time, no one would be allowed to flee. The weak would be crushed.

Trevor demanded silence. "You are part of a new order in this town. I officially proclaim Demon's Bluff under the control of the dark master, the night creatures. People like you!"

Whooping, hollering, and drunken laughter told him they were all for it. Of course they had no idea how real this was.

In the sky Trevor saw the heavy-lidded unblinking eyes. One day he would join them, the masters, the leaders. His reward awaited him.

Why couldn't these people smell the musk of the gathering herd overhead?

He led them in the cry, "Come to us! Come to us! Come to us!" A jagged flash cut the sky.

These people didn't matter. They comprised a mass, a stinking crowd of fattened animals ready to be led away. He would have his choice when the time came.

He would demand the honor of making the first offering.

THOSE POOR PEOPLE don't see the real Trevor like we do," Patch said, clearing a path. Few people wandered. Most had chosen a side—with Trevor or around the prayer rally fire.

Patch felt the gathering above, the low roar, the sharpening of swords. It was close and frightening. Would the Christians pray harder this time? Did God really want to watch a battle below? Patch couldn't guess what would happen.

"Go ahead, I'll catch up," Jarrod said, clearly annoyed. "Stupid crutches." He flung them away and crumbled.

Granger grabbed Jarrod on one side and signaled Patch to grab the other. But Jarrod flared. "I can manage myself." After a few seconds, he got himself under control and reached up.

"Just let us help," Granger said. "We want you there with us."

A change has come over Granger. Wonder if it's real? Patch chided himself for doubting.

With Nancy trailing and carrying Jarrod's crutches, the four scrambled to the edge of town, past the buildings, the tents, the rows of cars. The fire was glowing, flames twisting toward the skies.

"It's beautiful," Nancy said. "I hope Erin and Molly made it."

Always thinking of the others, Patch thought. He immediately felt guilty for his silent sarcasm. If he could change for the better, so could she.

They were almost there. Should he stop and tell everyone about Trevor's challenge, about the coming attack? They might run like last time, like in the painting at the museum.

He decided to leave it to God.

Erin and Molly had been wandering, looking for McCry, and they hadn't heard word one from Patch. Molly shook her walkie-talkie. "Maybe it's not working. We've been wasting our time."

"I hope it's broken," Erin said. "Otherwise Patch had better explain why he's been so rude. I've gone to bat for him more times than I can count."

"Let's head to the fire ring," Molly said, looking up. "Those clouds look weird." She shook her ponytail.

Erin agreed there was something ghostly about them—too low and strangely red.

45

WHAT'S THE CLAW doing here?" Patch said.

Granger shoved his hands into his pockets and shrugged. "Maybe she wants the truth."

"Or she's spying for Trevor," Patch said. He felt the old pain in his stomach, the warning that something bad was about to happen. He hadn't had so much as a twinge in days, but seeing Claudia set off a five-alarm fire. "She'll ruin everything."

Nancy said, "I won't have anything to do with her."

Patch noticed Nancy's set jaw and wondered if he looked that cruel.

"Fine," Jarrod said, snatching his crutches from Nancy without so much as a thank you. "You two sit somewhere else. I'm going to see how she's doing."

"Good idea," Granger said. "Me too."

"You lied to me, Granger," Nancy said, shaking, tears falling.

Patch had missed something, but he was sure curious. He pulled her toward a clearing a few yards away. Maybe Claudia *could* change. He chuckled. Yeah, if she could, anyone could.

Now he *did* feel cruel.

"What's wrong, Nancy?" Her skin was pale.

"Granger said he cared about me," she whispered. "Not Claudia. Now the second he sees her, he's off."

That reminded Patch of long-ago conversations with Molly, when she clearly wanted more than friendship. She couldn't understand how he could be concerned for her soul and nothing more.

"Maybe he's telling the truth. Give him a chance to explain. Prayer can change anyone."

I DON'T BELIEVE it," Erin said, seeing the crowds. "We're not going to find a place to sit."

They moved nearer the campfire and Molly froze.

"What's wrong?" Erin said, and then she saw. Claudia, four people back from the bonfire. Right in the middle.

"She can't stay," Molly said. "It's just wrong."

"Wait, Molly. Maybe God wants her here." Others shushed them, and Molly jostled free, taking off toward Claudia. Well, at least Granger and Jarrod were sitting next to her. Erin had a bad feeling.

Claudia howled as Molly grabbed her and tried to pull her to her feet.

Pastor Ron motioned for the people to stop singing and signaled Jarrod to keep things calm.

All eyes focused on them.

"Molly, let's talk this out later," Jarrod said, looking up.

"Don't you know who she is? Or what she is?"

Jarrod stood and leaned on his crutches. "Fine, we'll deal with this right now." He put a hand on Molly's shoulder, but she swept it off and Jarrod lost his balance and fell. He struggled to his feet. "I'm fine. Claudia, do you want to stay?"

Granger held Molly back. Claudia's face was white, her blonde hair tangled.

Molly pushed away from Granger. "You're one of the liars. I've seen what you do to Christians."

"This is a prayer rally," Pastor Ron said. "Clearly, we need more of it." People calmed down, sat, and Jarrod followed Granger, Molly, and Claudia out.

Ahead, Patch and Nancy moved away. From another angle came Erin. The whole gang was here.

GRANGER LAGGED, WATCHING. Where did Molly get off treating Claudia that way? She hadn't even let the Claw explain. Maybe Patch's crowd wasn't where he wanted to be.

Sure, prayer worked sometimes. After all, he'd been able to yank the ring off. But all this conflict over God? He didn't think it was worth the hassle.

Granger stayed in the shadows as they hurried past. He wanted no part of their squabble. It wasn't his battle.

NANCY, I DON'T know what's wrong," Patch said. The face of that pointy, dust-coated rat came to mind. His bite wound was burning

so badly he could hardly stand. He needed to rest and ice it.
Maybe he needed stronger medicine.

"What's wrong with you?" The old clawing Claudia. Her voice
scraped like a razor.

Patch told her what had happened to him.

"Maybe it's infected," Erin said.

"I'll be fine."

They moved toward the church. Patch felt faint. The burning
spread up from his calf.

"He needs help," Nancy said.

Molly looked about to explode. "What can I do?"

Patch reached for her hand. It felt cool but her brow showed
worry.

"Get a doctor to the church," he managed. And he fell.

46

MOLLY PUSHED THROUGH the crowd, thrilled to be alone, away from those wafflers. Couldn't make a decision to save their souls. Well, she could. Thank goodness Patch had given her something to do, a task.

The pastor. They'd barely met at the church, but she didn't care. Patch was sick, maybe real sick. The pastor had to know a doctor, someone who could help.

A man came out of nowhere. Molly neared the front of the fire circle. She shrugged his hand off her shoulder. "Leave me alone. My friend was hurt, and I have to—"

"Hurt by your words, no doubt."

He thought she meant Claudia.

"No, she's not my friend." That didn't come out right.

"Obviously."

This wasn't working. She had to get away. The pastor was

speaking about how the world knows we care by the way we love each other. The words stabbed.

She didn't care about Claudia. Hate was all she felt toward her. She'd been through a lot of bad times, many caused by the Claw. Claudia didn't care about anyone but herself.

Just like me.

Molly stopped in her tracks, convicted. "I'm sorry, sir. You're right. That must have looked horrible. Claudia and I have a long history. I'll make that right, but now I have to get help for a friend who was bitten by an animal." Molly begged him to talk to the pastor, send someone to the church to help.

"Sure, when it's over I'll check with him."

"No!" Molly shouted. "Let me go!" Molly stomped through the darkness, the aisle widening as she passed. "He needs help now. I didn't make this up."

Before she realized it she was walking into town, toward the lights and sound of the Spirit Fest. Maybe the people she couldn't imagine helping would surprise her.

Trevor had power. She had seen it. Maybe he'd help Patch. Who cared, as long as Patch got better? She was realistic. What worked, worked. Even if you didn't know why.

The beat of the music drew her. All she could think about was helping her friend. Why not use Trevor for God's purpose? Was that even possible? Patch always said God used for good the things man intends for evil. And Trevor brought new meaning to the word.

Closer to the packed courthouse, the lawn was filled with people chanting, "Come to us! Come to us!"

Maybe this wasn't such a good idea. Trevor stood fewer than a hundred feet from her, on stage under the lights. He looked like a rock star, stirring the crowd.

He was one handsome guy. Maybe he would heal Patch to show off. Something inside her heart made her question that thought. She pushed her worry aside. The excitement, the sounds. This place rocked.

Suddenly lights began dropping from the sky like comets, smashing into the ground around the stage. From the center of each arose winged creatures, white and shining—beautiful as angels, their eyes gleaming.

Molly was thrilled. These couldn't be demons. They came from above, dressed in white, lit from within.

These had to be the good guys.

GRANGER WATCHED THE soaring lights falling from the sky toward the concert. Something was happening and he wanted to find out what. He headed for the church.

Better to hang out with the others than be bored all alone.

Anyway, the jury was still out. Prayer or power. From the looks of it you either got one or the other. Never both.

So Granger would check things out. See what happened. Then decide. He jammed his hands into his pockets and hurried down the street.

47

WHERE IS SHE?" Erin went to the door again, looked up and down the streets for Molly. Patch needed help, and fast.

"That girl has never liked me," Claudia said.

"That's hardly the point right now, but as long as you brought it up, what were you doing at the rally?"

"Checking out the competition," Claudia said, seeming to force a smile. "No, seriously, you want the truth? There was this little girl . . ." She told Erin about seeing the child praying, appearing so sure of herself, certain she was talking to God. "Really made me think. I'm afraid."

"We all are," Patch said. "Spiritual warfare separates the believers from the undecided."

"You haven't seen what Trevor can do. I have. So has Nancy."

What? Either Nancy knew more than she was saying, or Claudia was lying.

PATCH'S FEVER SHOWED on his face, sweat pouring from his hairline. Nancy patted him with a wet kitchen towel.

Jarrod looked at the clock. Molly should have brought a doctor by now. The teeth marks had scabbed over and the wound bulged.

"We have to do something."

"We've been praying," Granger said. "Not that it's helping."

Jarrod didn't like Granger's attitude. The guy had arrived almost thirty minutes after the rest of them. "Where've you been?"

"Back off. I'm not the spiritual one." His long neck was flushed. "I don't answer to you."

"I'm going to go find a doctor myself," Jarrod said. "I'll make an announcement in front of the whole group if I have to. Nancy, keep Patch cool and give him as much water as he'll take."

THE CLEARLY AWED crowd quieted as the white-winged creatures floated toward Trevor, then bounded onto the stage. He appeared to be controlling them. That's what he wanted.

His arm muscles bulged and stretched his costume. Something had to give. Either he'd have to let everyone see his real self, or he'd have to calm down.

Turning back wasn't an option.

Three shining beings stood to his right, three others to his left. Trevor reached toward them, and they too began chanting, "Come to us."

"More angels?" someone in the crowd shouted.

The crowd, no longer cowering, moved closer, plainly intrigued.

Wait until the masks come off. Trevor sensed hordes above the clouds. Ready. He was in control. The world hung in space because he said so. If only he had someone to share the moment with.

Then he saw a familiar face: Molly, his old friend.

She had that look about her, as if his magic entwined her. He wanted her near. He reached toward her and forced her to step closer. She didn't even try to resist. Why would she? He was the prize.

JARROD HOBBLED ALONG, hearing the screaming. "Come to us!" Louder, frantic. Trevor's show was only a block away. Did Jarrod dare check it out? The more information the better. But Patch needed help now.

He should head straight for the prayer circle. No detours.

Suddenly Jarrod's feet tingled with warmth. Was it the ground? No. It was . . . It was his feet! He stopped, amazed, as he realized what was happening. His toes tingled.

He dropped his crutches and took a step. And another. A miracle. He wasn't hobbling.

He could walk! He could leap!

God was at the prayer rally. God was here. God was everywhere.

But if this was a miracle why didn't Jarrod feel like praying? He didn't even care to acknowledge God's gift to him. His mind, his body told him to give up, give in, step closer to the stage. The music, the voices, pulled him closer.

But those towering beings were calling for someone, something. Jarrod knew in his heart that this was a trap. They were trying to bring evil to earth.

Jarrod forced himself to pray. "Take me from this temptation. Help me." He didn't stop his torrent of words.

He turned to run, but with his first step he crashed.

So it was true. God had not given him strength. Something else had. A false force had healed him. Now Jarrod's legs hurt. He crawled to the crutches and struggled to his feet. He had to get to the fire circle and Pastor Ron.

MOLLY SLOGGED TOWARD the stage, toward Trevor. What a nice smile. She couldn't help returning it. A force pulled her toward him.

Why wouldn't he let her come on her own power? Did he have to drag people to his side? They'd come on their own. That's what she felt like doing.

The crowd opened for her, big grins, wide eyes, chanting, "Come to us. Come to us. Come to us."

Trevor reached for her, and she was on stage taking his hand. He wouldn't hurt her. So handsome, like he'd stepped off the cover of a magazine.

Molly felt like a prom queen. It was nice, all the applause.

48

JARROD HAD LEFT, and Molly had not come back. Patch was worse. Erin couldn't stand seeing him in pain. The concrete courtyard outside the church provided a place for her to stretch.

Claudia and Nancy had followed her out. Although Nancy kept to herself, Claudia was driving Erin crazy with her chatter. She was going on about Nancy and the demons again. Could Claudia be telling the truth? Maybe Nancy did have a secret.

Bored with Claudia's talking, Erin led the way back inside. Granger, long face clouded, pointed out the window. "See how light it's getting? Pink as dawn." It was an observation. He didn't act like he cared much either way.

"It's too early for that. The prayer rally will go all night."

"Prayer." Claudia put a hand on her hip. "Like that's done any good."

Erin saw Granger nod his agreement.

TREVOR PUT HIS arm around Molly. Tall, thin, flawless. Who wouldn't want to be close to her? And that smile, her thick brown hair. This was perfect.

He saw adoration in the crowd's eyes. For him, for her, for them.

The beings on either side of Trevor weren't having as much fun. "Get on with it," one grumbled. "Give the word." More muttering.

"It's not time," Trevor hissed, mouth behind his hand. "Play nice for a few more minutes."

The gleaming soldiers raised their arms. "Come to us!" Their deep voices shook the sky, cracked sidewalks. People dropped to their knees, covered their heads.

That's more like it. Trevor was almost ready.

Soon the masks would fall.

ERIN KNEW THAT God didn't always give the answers she wanted, but this was a miracle. It seemed God had removed the poison from Patch's body. She was thankful.

Patch looked stronger. The swelling was gone, the red replaced by a pale pink.

"You feel cooler," Nancy said.

"Where are the others?" Patch asked.

"Jarrod's getting help; we don't know about Molly," Erin said.

"We think she went over to . . . the enemy," Claudia said. After a look at Claudia, Erin nodded.

Nancy looked at both of them. Confession time.

She told of seeing Trevor transform into a demon, huge and strong, and how he made McCry and Frazier disappear. "You should know what we're dealing with."

Something in Claudia's expression snapped, changed. She nodded. "Believe me, girl, we know what we're dealing with. We're dealing with a psycho liar. You're making all this up to yank the spotlight back on yourself. Pathetic."

Nancy stared at Claudia with a mixture of confusion and loathing. Erin couldn't believe Nancy would make this up. Knowing Trevor, this could all be true. "So you're saying none of this happened?"

Claudia cracked her knuckles. "She's a liar. Always has been." She pushed her blonde hair back.

"Then where are they?" Erin said. "McCry has been tracking us for miles. Surely she'd have found us by now."

With a shrug, Claudia walked out.

49

IT WAS TIME. Trevor clamped tighter onto Molly's hand and saw her fear. Good.

Several on the edge of the crowd looked ready to run. Trevor pointed at them and they fell on their faces, crying. Perfect.

Trevor reached behind his head and located the release point beneath his hairline. The mask split, slipped up and over his long snout, and popped past his steaming nostrils.

Molly gasped as Trevor's costume fell away. Impressed, he was sure. They always were.

JARROD PLANTED HIS legs and raised a crutch to get Pastor Ron's attention. "It is time. The enemy will attack soon."

Questions popped like corn in a kettle.

"What?"

"What do you mean?"

"Where?"

"My children," another cried. "We've got to get out of here."

Jarrod knew hysteria might break out, almost expected it. Just as was portrayed in the museum painting. "Stop!" he shouted. "That's what they want, to scare us and divide us."

The pastor welcomed him forward and held the mike for him.

"I threw these crutches down tonight. Healed."

"Praise God!" The voices raised in joy. Jarrod calmed them with a movement of his open hand.

"No. It wasn't God. The enemy gave me the strength to walk, but only for one purpose—to move toward their evil. But I refused. I will not walk if it means rejecting Jesus."

Jarrod paused in the eerie silence. "We must pray as we've never prayed before. Evil forces will be upon us unless we pray now."

Jarrod knelt, his eyes closed.

50

SOMEONE SHOULD GO after Claudia," Patch said. "Someone needs to talk to her, see where she really stands."

"She made her choice." Erin said. "She's probably hot on Trevor's trail."

Patch swung his legs to the side and felt a blackness cover him like a bag. "I'll go after her."

Erin sighed and pushed him down. "Rest. I'll get her."

Nancy whispered to Granger, and he left with Erin.

Patch leaned back. Maybe there was a chance for Claudia.

TREVOR HAD MORPHED into a monster from one of Molly's darkest dreams.

And she knew why. At least she grasped how she'd gotten herself in such a mess. She had stopped praying, let doubts pick their way into her mind. Now she needed to free herself. But Trevor's grip was like steel. The things on stage with her leered and drooled.

She'd been sucked in by the lights, the show. Molly stopped pulling, and Trevor loosened his hold. If she just kept still enough to keep his attention off her . . .

People ran, terror on their faces. Some hid behind trees. Trevor raised his hands and yanked them back, flying, shouting as they hit the ground.

With a lurch, Molly jumped off the stage and raced toward the courthouse.

THE SHINING ONE and the Radiant One stood waiting for the trumpet blast that would trigger the battle.

"They must keep praying." The Shining One said. "Their fire grows dim."

CLAUDIA HAD GONE hardly half a block when Erin and Granger caught her. Erin was sick of the games. She leaned into Claudia's face. "Patch says we should try to save the Claw. Don't know why."

"Don't call me that. And what, can't you believe someone like me could change?"

Claudia had tears in her eyes. *More acting,* Erin decided.

"Okay," Claudia said. "Nancy told the truth about Trevor. But I wanted to be the one to tell the story. Is that wrong?"

What a stupid excuse. *Oh, brother,* Erin thought. "Always fun to be the one in the know," she said. Of course she couldn't count the times she herself had doled out gossip like gold.

"Trevor is dangerous," Claudia said. "We have to find Molly."

Someone ran past, muttering that they should get out, get away. Claudia gingerly fingered her necklace. "Shining evil," she said. "Lets me peek into people's minds."

"Get rid of it," Granger said. "Bury it." Erin thought he sounded angry.

A group thundered past, just missing Erin.

Claudia turned ashen and wrapped the necklace in a cloth. "One of those guys had a picture of a girl in his mind." She ran toward the noise, toward the spotlights, calling over her shoulder, "She was on stage with Trevor! I think it was Molly!"

For a split second, Erin stared after Claudia in amazement. Then, with a shrug, she ran after her, Granger loping behind. Claudia was crazy. So was she for following her.

Ahead, on the stage, glowing white blobs oozed on either side of a winged monster, jaws wide, tail reaching thirty feet. Erin knew she could be smashed by it.

Claudia ran screaming like a wild woman. "Trevor!"

JARROD WANTED TO be with Patch, but he felt better knowing the doctor was on his way. In the meantime Jarrod could do more on his knees.

Angels' wings. No one had to tell Jarrod. He could see their faces, their strong bodies wrapped in the whitest linen, armor shining. Swords were raised as the army streamed by. Too many to count.

Jarrod had never seen such a sight. He wanted to chase after them. But his place was here, praying. He squeezed his eyelids tighter.

51

THE DOOR TO the courthouse was locked.

All Trevor had to do was look Molly's way and reach for her. She turned and felt her way along the wall, moving toward the edge of the building. If she could get around to the side, she could run. Until then she was exposed.

Too late. Trevor's bulging eyes found her. His raised his fist, and Molly covered her ears at his rage. Her head flung back, her stomach pressing her spine, she hit the brick wall and slumped to the concrete. She skidded along on her back, arms reaching for something, anything to grab onto.

"God help me," she whispered as she slipped through the grass. In seconds she'd be in Trevor's grasp.

She put her feet out as if on a sled and let them slide beneath the short curtain that rimmed the platform. She disappeared below Trevor and heard screams. Someone had stolen Trevor's attention.

ERIN WATCHED, PARALYZED as Claudia swung back and forth on Trevor's tail.

"Help her, Granger!"

"No way." He stepped behind a tree. Refused to help.

Erin was furious. The white demons swayed and emitted ghoulish laughter.

Claudia had been insane to leap onto the beast. Or she was the bravest person Erin had ever seen.

She spied Molly peeking out from under the front of the stage. Trevor's tail hit the edge of the platform as Claudia hung on, teeth clenched, eyes closed.

Erin knew what she had to do: grab Molly and get out of there.

She ran toward Molly. "Molly! Over here!" But Molly wouldn't leave Claudia.

Okay, then she would help Claudia, make up for her rotten attitude. No more fear, no more running.

Erin ran for Trevor, Molly right behind her. They leapt aboard the thrashing tail. The three of them, working together, pinned Trevor to the stage. His strength seeped out and Trevor shrank. There was no way to explain it. He was their size now, eye to eye, puny biceps, little bird claws, scrawny wings.

Trevor snatched up his costume and ran.

GRANGER WATCHED MOLLY and Erin helping Claudia. He should help, do something, but how were they his problem? They'd gotten themselves into this whole thing. And it looked like they were winning—for now. All they had to do was pray, right?

Granger checked his pocket.

The ring was still there. Ready whenever he needed it.

I SENSE DARKNESS rising," Pastor Ron thundered. "Keep praying."

Jarrod imagined angels, faces grim, tearing toward battle.

"Pray for those under temptation, for those fighting evil, one-on-one."

Jarrod did. Harder than ever.

52

THE RADIANT ONE leaned back on a rooftop near where the Shining One sat. They listened as Claudia raged.

"He used me, lied to me." Claudia balled up the silver necklace and flung it skyward. "How could I ever believe he'd give a gift worth keeping?"

As the girl roared on, Erin led the trio to the church.

The Radiant One pointed toward the red clouds, low, rolling. Lightning zigzagged.

"They'll be here soon."

"Keep praying."

AS THEY NEARED the church, Claudia's legs failed and she slid to the ground. "I didn't know."

"Didn't know what?" Erin asked as she and Molly helped Claudia up.

"How could I? I've never seen God answer me before," Claudia said. "I didn't know what would happen if I prayed."

Erin had to give Claudia credit. Never in a hundred summers would she have dived for a demon's tail if she hadn't seen the Claw tackling the impossible.

"You were incredible."

Claudia shook her head. "No. God was."

THE PASTOR POINTED overhead. Jarrod was stunned. Everyone looked. The red sky appeared to droop. It looked full of some writhing thing—something that wanted out.

Shouts, confusion.

"Should we run?"

"Stay right where you are." The pastor raised both hands. "But keep looking, keep watching."

Jarrod was going to get his wish to be part of something huge. He wondered how Patch and the others were. Wherever they were, he hoped they were praying.

PATCH STOOD AT the doorway, his arm around Erin's shoulder. The swelling was gone, the pain a memory. He had no fever. He wanted back in the thick of things.

"Just rest." Nancy pushed a cool cloth to his forehead.

Patch swatted her away. "I'm sick of sitting."

Erin said, "So that's all the thanks he gets?"

"He?"

Erin smiled. "God."

Heart full, Patch apologized for being a brat. He'd have his chance to get into the action, but first God deserved his gratitude.

Y OU SHOULD HAVE been nicer to us." Trevor recognized the voice. Demon Girl was back, but not as Hope. Her hide was wrinkled, smelly, her claws sharp and long. Her eyes stuck out like a bug's and her noseless face was pinched, ancient looking.

"Yeah," Demon Guy said. Except he didn't look like a harmless teen named Barry. No longer was he fearful. He leaned over Trevor, his bulky, muscular body broad and sweaty. Trevor was no match for this beast. Maybe he never had been.

"I was trying to toughen you two up," the disgraced demon moaned. "It was for your own good." He tried to shout but could barely speak above a whisper. He was afraid as never before.

The two circled Trevor. His costume was heaped at his feet, his demonic arms weak, small. Chains bound each wrist. Yanking, he tried to free himself. The metal shuddered, clattered.

"This is for *your* own good," Demon Girl said, laughing. She grabbed her cohort's twisted paw and ran.

What was to happen to him now? Trevor wished he *had* been nicer to them. He was sure word had spread about his zapping them back to this world beyond time.

His old teacher Flabbygums hunched near him, smelling of rotted garbage. Trevor had missed the scents of home, the eternal fire pit at the edge of the abyss—that burning hole impossible to escape where worthless demons were tossed to scream and scratch.

He looked behind him at the spitting flames. Hungry for him, eager to devour his weakness.

"You've done it again, haven't you?" his teacher said, wielding a stick, at the top of which swung a small, dirty cage.

Trevor tugged at his chains. The old being loosed Trevor.

Maybe he could talk his way into another chance. "I've got an idea," Trevor said.

"One that'll work this time?" Flabbygums eyed him as a child does an ice cream cone.

"It almost worked."

The teacher growled. "'Almost worked' means 'completely failed.' But all is not lost. We can still use you. A new wave flies out soon. Since you know the town best, you're going with them."

"Happy to lead," Trevor said.

"You're going in a cage. As an example."

What? Trevor felt a terrible tearing that gripped from within. In an instant, his bones had shriveled, his skin tightened. He was suddenly tiny enough to roost in a bird cage. Before he could fly away, Mr. Flabbygums snatched him and flung him into the little prison.

Trevor held on as the cage banged into the stick when Flabby-gums plodded along.

"Look at the birdie."

"Yeah, the puny birdie." The Demonic Duo was back, poking at him with long jagged finger-claws. "Scary."

They could crush him. He flitted around the cage, out of their grasp. "Stop it!" he squeaked, then slapped a hand over his mouth. He sounded silly. Certainly nothing to be afraid of.

"Does the little thing want some birdseed?" Demon Girl said.

Demon Guy released a silt of crushed rocks and metal chunks over his cage. "Eat up," he said.

Trevor covered his exposed head with his frail wings. He coughed in the dusty din.

"Let him be," Flabbygums said. "You'll have more time to play later."

53

CLAUDIA, MOLLY, WHAT are you doing here?" Jarrod said, but he had to admit they looked ready to wrestle a crocodile, sweaty faces all smiles.

"If this is where people pray," Claudia said, "then I belong here."

"You can pray anywhere, any time," Jarrod said. "But we're glad you're here."

All around them people prayed, some quietly, all with power. This was incredible. No turn taking; each talked to God one-on-one.

Jarrod beamed. God was moving, changing hearts. Something huge was happening, and he was part of it.

"Look." A young man pointed. "In the sky."

Jarrod saw eyes of hatred. Demons glowing, growing. More and more of them.

This was war. The enemy had the high ground, the sky. Where

were those angels, their angels? Why weren't they here? Fear crept from his head to his feet.

"Maybe we'd better leave," he said, suddenly feeling isolated and weak. Clumps of prayer warriors were scattering, people on the edges moved away. Jarrod beckoned to his friends. "Let's go."

"Never." Claudia said, firm as bedrock. "I know which side I'm on. I'm staying."

"Me too," Molly said. "I'm not afraid."

Molly reached for Jarrod, but he was afraid to take her hand. The huge faces loomed, the sky a screen of terrors beyond anything he'd ever imagined.

Jarrod wanted to be brave, but he wasn't going to be stupid.

He leaned hard on his crutches, ready to flee.

Let's go," Patch said, pacing. "I'm fine now." He wanted up, out, anywhere but here.

Nancy leaned against the wall, watching. "Coming?" Erin asked.

She shook her head. "I'll hang around in case they come back."

"We might need you," Patch said.

"I'm not ready to leave this place yet." Nancy knit her hands together.

Patch thought he heard Erin say "oh, brother." He didn't blame her. Let Nancy be a coward. He and the others would find and follow God's will. Nancy would miss out.

But before they could get far, Patch was stopped by a stampede, as if the whole town were running.

Not again.

"Stop!" Patch screamed. Nancy came outside, and she and Erin held Patch back. "Don't they realize what they're doing?"

Nancy mumbled, "They're afraid, Patch." She let go of him. "Just like we are."

Erin pulled Patch inside the church. People tromped in, clearly frightened, looking for places to hide. The pews began to fill with cowering families.

Patch sighed. "Prayer was supposed to be the answer."

"Well, how many prayer warriors do we need?" Erin said. "There's you and me. And Nancy."

He got it. God would listen—and act—even if only one bothered to pray.

But Nancy wasn't with them. She moved from person to person, handing out water. She seemed content to play the role of waitress. Patch wanted to shake her, to shout at her to come over, really help.

He finally turned his back on her and her sweet smile and calm voice. Let her stay. He and Erin were going to do something.

GRANGER PEERED IN through the window. Nancy was there. He felt foolish for worrying, but she was all he cared about. The only person worth saving.

The place was packed. Frightened faces, crying kids. What a mess. How could she stay so calm in the middle of chaos? He admired her.

He should help. But, no. They weren't his problem.

Granger wanted no part of this. As long as his Nancy was safe, that's all that mattered.

54

NANCY COULDN'T LEAVE the sanctuary. Not that she wanted to.
The others probably thought her a coward. But this was where she
was supposed to be. Nancy's prayers poured out, spurred by each anxious face. Through tidbits of news, she understood what was happening outside.

But she was afraid to scan the skies herself.

Better to stay here, helping, praying quietly.

There wasn't anything wrong with that, was there?

Where was Granger? She was scared for him. She even prayed
for Claudia. That was right, good. What God wanted her to do.

CLAUDIA WATCHED JARROD hobble away. She turned to Molly.
"Just us two?"

"And me." Another voice, and another. At least a dozen. Pastor Ron called them closer.

"Even if there was only one man or woman praying, God would hear and answer." Pastor Ron reached out, gathered the others into an intimate prayer circle.

"God, we need you," Claudia began. Others poured out words through tears. Claudia refused to open her eyes, refused to let the leering faces above terrify her. So what if there were more of them, and they were bigger? She would keep praying no matter what.

JARROD'S CRUTCHES HAD been crushed to splinters by frightened feet. Why had he run?

Because he was afraid. And now he was alone. In the dark.

He rolled onto his back. The stars were gone, crowded out by demon eyes, mouths, faces. Staring at him. Jarrod turned over, struggled to his knees.

Why did he waffle? How come he could never stick to his guns long enough to make a difference?

He knew the answer. Fear crept in when trust shriveled due to lack of prayer.

Time to get serious again. He had screwed up, but that was no reason to abandon the God who would never abandon him. Jarrod bowed his head. He couldn't walk, couldn't hide. But he could pray.

STOP, PATCH!" ERIN screamed. "There's no point!"

He knew she was right, but he didn't want to hear it. He was standing on tiptoe, certain he could poke a finger in the eye of a squirming, grunting demon. The sky was full, dripping with visions that curdled his stomach, sounds that clanked. Howling wolves couldn't compare to a demon choir.

Patch could hardly hear his thoughts.

No matter where he went, he could see enormous faces, smell their putrid breath. He took Erin's hand. "You afraid?"

"Terrified."

"So am I. That's why we're going to stay right where we are and stare these monsters down."

TREVOR'S SKINNY LITTLE body was perched, shivering, on a small swing in the cage. His demonic kin were ready to rip people apart. And all he could do was watch. He saw his tormenters leer at him. Demon Girl and Guy would get in on the fun. He was furious.

All those huge monsters blocked his vision. He was stuck in the back with the weaklings, the washouts, the worthless.

Wasn't he the one who'd gotten them here? They should show a little respect. Trevor hopped off his swing, trotted to the cage door, and lifted the lever. Someone had forgotten to lock it. Good thing he'd thought to check.

He was free. His wings were flimsy as a fly's, but maybe he could make it to the action. No one would even notice him. He could stand with the warriors, earn his size and strength back by attacking the few remaining creatures who dared stay to pray.

As he flew in the shadows he felt his eyes sharpen, his wings grow, his body swelling. It was working. The Father of Lies was honoring him, giving him back the power that had been stolen.

The Demon Duo he'd trained would learn a lesson from the master.

Trevor smiled as he landed, large as a raptor, quiet as a cat. He limped behind a tall building and waited. Before long he'd grown to where he could peer over the roof. Where was everybody? Probably shivering in terror of him like Flabbygums taught.

Trevor planned to find his former classmates and teach them some lessons about terror. He could hardly wait to taste Patrick's fear. Oh, yeah, this was going to be his night.

He still felt shaky, unsteady. His budding wings flapped in spurts, not working right. That didn't matter. He could lumber along until every component had healed.

Hide. Don't let them see you coming.

But he had places to go. First he'd stop at the white-washed church where the Christians would hide.

55

CLAUDIA WAS ON board for a whopping battle, but could she be dead certain she'd chosen the right side?

Trevor had ripped Ms. McCry and Ms. Frazier out of time and space, but he had also given Claudia the power to know the thoughts of others.

Remembering made her smile. What a rush. No wonder people wanted the extras that came with compromise. But she also knew there was a price for accepting those rewards.

Her soul. It was as real as the blood-red evil hovering over their heads. Satan hated her, wanted to tempt her. As much as the old Claudia might have wavered, the new Claudia was different.

She stood when others had fallen. She led the battle against a demon the size of a school bus. No more back and forth. Her choice was made: God all the way.

PATCH AND ERIN finally made it back to the prayer rally.

Maybe Nancy was as solidly on God's team as he was. He'd never taken the time to talk to her, just long-jumped from conclusion to conclusion. He owed it to her to give her a chance.

Where had Granger gone?

Pray, Patch. Now.

Get focused. Be ready when God needs you.

56

NANCY STARED UP at the tearing sound as the church separated at the roof line. Claws picked at it as though working on cardboard.

She'd been praying, trying to help the frightened. She did whatever she could, as she had learned as hospital volunteer.

But now this. Screams sounded near, loud. Tears flooded her eyes.

So much for her newborn faith. Nancy fell to the floor and watched her world rip apart. Windows shattered, revealing the red sky. The eye of the demon did not blink, and Nancy recognized him.

How many times would she have to deal with this monster Trevor? She knew she had to get up and do something. The others didn't know, couldn't know, what this demon was capable of.

Children huddled against their parents, adults covered their eyes. Nancy stood. So what if Trevor saw her fear? She was afraid. What was wrong with that? Most people never saw a demon; Nancy went to school with one.

Trevor screeched and roared, and many slipped out through windows and side doors. Soon Nancy would be alone, exactly as she wanted.

Ceiling chunks and paint flecks fell like snow. Nancy covered her head, pushed hair from her eyes, and waited.

Trevor clawed at the corner like a rat trying to eat its way through a box of cookies. His monstrous mouth chewed slowly through the bricks.

She didn't care.

"I'm no longer afraid, Trevor," she said.

He shook his mighty mouth and squeezed his head inside. Football-sized eyes stared, jaws clanked.

"I used to think you were stronger, Trevor. My mistake."

Trevor coughed as if something had lodged in his throat. His big head disappeared. What had happened to him? Nancy yanked open the door.

He wasn't going to get away that easy.

THE SHINING ONE'S assistant looked as anxious as he sounded. "There are more of them than there are of us." The sky was a patchwork of red mixed with orange and dark purple, stitched together with strands of black. A demon quilt.

"God's waiting."

The assistant heard the trumpet from the Shining One as he swooped by.

Finally. It was time for the battle.

Unless God had something else in mind.

MOLLY'S EYES SHONE. How could she be so happy in a situation like this? Claudia was mad.

"Isn't there something we can *do?*" Claudia said, interrupting what was left of the prayer rally and causing the pastor's eyes to pop open. No doubt he'd recommend more prayer.

The shrieking demon choir filled her ears, the noise an exclamation point to the Pastor's words. "Our prayer keeps the devils above at bay." With Claudia's interruption, they let loose their roaring.

That made her decision easy. She wasn't going to stop praying until this thing was over.

Their prayers stopped the mouths of the chattering demons, and the silence was sweet. But they were clearly waiting for another opening. If Claudia had anything to do with it, there wouldn't be one.

57

ERIN STARED OVER Patch's shoulder, mouth agape, as Patch turned. This wasn't going to be good.

The thing stomped toward them, but something was wrong with this one. "It's tipping," Patch said.

Erin jerked Patch to his feet. The ground shook when the creature landed full on its face.

"Run!"

The heavy-legged thing pulled itself up on the sides of buildings with scrawny front claws. He tottered, righted himself. Scurried on.

Patch prayed as he ran, then snuck a glance over his shoulder. The demon was gaining, huge feet flying, making the sidewalk bounce.

"Erin, stop!" She skidded to a halt and they turned to face the creature.

The demon used his tail as an anchor, dust flying off the spiny tip.

What? The demon had stopped, too, just as he was about to overtake his prey? This made no sense.

"Guess it's time." Patch raised his palms. "It's you, isn't it?"

"Is it that obvious?" Trevor bellowed.

"Don't you ever get tired of this?" Patch said as Erin inched toward him. They had no weapons, nothing but prayer.

Trevor tripped and lurched.

"Feet too big for you?" Patch said. He was finally getting it. "You can be hurt if God's people aren't afraid of you."

Trevor the demon pointed to spectators cowering behind windows. "Looks like a bunch of weaklings." His voice rattled the windows.

"If it isn't the biggest bird on the block."

What? It was Nancy. What was she doing here?

"Looks like something out of a cheap monster movie," she said, "but he's only an oversized chicken." Nancy flapped her arms and clucked as she danced.

This wasn't the same Nancy Patch had left at the church. She was wild, unafraid.

"Careful, Nancy," Erin said. "He'll hurt you."

Nancy bowed her head. "God, take away their terror. Let them see this thing for what he really is."

Trevor transformed before them, becoming small, weak, gasping. Patch lost his fear.

"How did you know?" Patch said, as Trevor fell hard, bending his tail.

"I prayed him away a while ago," she said. "Amazing what we can do when we stop being afraid."

Erin hugged Nancy. "Let's find Jarrod and the others."

JARROD HEARD FOOTSTEPS. No sense sitting there in the dark if someone was around. "Help! Over here."

"That you, Jarrod? It's your old friend."

Relief welled up, and Jarrod knew he was going to be okay. Then he saw it. Some kind of a freaky creature, a scrawny Tyrannosaurus Rex. A turkey on stilts. He smelled the foul breath when it opened its jaws.

DO YOU HEAR that, Molly?" Claudia said. She'd heard something about a hundred yards off, like an animal in pain.

Molly used her flashlight as they picked their way toward the sounds, finally coming upon Jarrod beating up the demon. His limp legs whipped from side to side as he held Trevor's neck.

"Get out of here!" Claudia shouted, raising a fist to Trevor. "Leave my friend alone." The creature clomped away as though wearing wooden shoes. He didn't look back.

Molly and Claudia carried Jarrod back to the rally where Patch and Erin met them.

58

W HAT A MESS. Another horrible mistake.

Trevor limped along, aching. But hadn't he tried? He had been brave enough to go back, but what good had that done him? He was weakening again, getting smaller. If things didn't change he'd end up living in a cage with Hope and Barry as zookeepers.

What a nightmare.

Nothing had gone his way. Hordes of demons awaited the signal from the Father of Lies. He should be aligned with the conquering heroes above rather than wandering the desert looking for his costume. But he had to find it. It was his only chance. Trevor didn't want anyone else seeing him this way, emaciated.

Trevor pawed the rocky soil. Where had he left it? That's right, over there, in a tangle of branches.

It turned out to be a huge rat's nest. When he knelt, a long pointy rodent nose nearly touched his own. It fussed at him before scurrying off.

With his stubby front legs, Trevor clawed at the branches until he found the sturdy canvas bag and in it his human shell.

The costume fit loosely, but at least he had survived. All he had to do now was find a ride out of town. He couldn't risk going back for his own car.

The highway lay at the base of the bluff. He slid his way down.

When the first car slowed, Trevor worked the muscles in his face to make himself look sad. *If they feel sorry for you, you can get them to do anything.* This was going to be easy.

The back door popped open and Trevor climbed in. "Thanks so much," he said in his most timid voice.

"Happy to help, Trevor."

McCry. Just his luck. Now what was he supposed to do?

Pastor Ron looked over Patch's group. "In case you haven't noticed, we're not all here. Many are missing. While we can rejoice over our own safety, let's not forget those who are still out there somewhere."

As the night cooled, the pastor had them build a small fire. Patch sat near it, feeling weak as a newborn puppy. Claudia's face was full of expectation, but her eyes were tired. Nancy appeared about to fall asleep. Erin and Molly were praying. Jarrod seemed alert, probably still wired from fighting Trevor. Where had Granger wandered off to?

The prayer rally hadn't gone as Patch planned. But when was the last time anything went his way?

The waiting strained his patience. Let the clouds crack. Let the demons fall.

Let this be done.

THE SHINING ONE was sure. "The sky is ripe with demons ready to drop. It'll be like a hailstorm." Before their release every man, woman, and child in Demon's Bluff must be accounted for.

In a visible human body the Shining One knocked at the church door. A man with matted hair peeked out. "What do you want?" he said, fear in his eyes.

"God has questions for you." The man tried to slam the door shut but the Shining One caught the edge, easily pushed it wide, and stepped inside.

59

WHAT WERE THE odds? Having Trevor in her backseat made McCry's day. She kept an eye on him in her rearview mirror. "Don't even think about it. You can't unlock it from the inside."

His smug expression was gone. "We can work something out," he said.

McCry snorted. "You're right about that." She didn't want him to know how scared she was. One moment she had been in his hotel room in the middle of town and the next in her own home.

Frazier had sworn her to secrecy. She knew how that would look, their both having been terrorized by a demon. Frazier had also ordered McCry back to Demon's Bluff. Neither would have dreamed of this coincidence: Trevor as a hitchhiker.

"You didn't expect me to return, did you?"

"Oh, I was hoping to see you again."

McCry snorted. He did have a wicked sense of humor.

She couldn't let Trevor escape. He was too valuable, had too many secrets hidden in that skull. Plus power. He wasn't much to look at now, but he had sent her and Frazier flying from his room. If she could somehow harness that, imagine using it against law-breakers. Troublemakers would be things of the past. Literally.

Trevor would show her his secrets. McCry would make him.

McCry drove into town and parked near the hotel where the tattered remains of the stage stood.

"Let me out!" Trevor said, banging on the headrest.

"You don't scare me," she said, applying plastic cuffs from the glove compartment and jerking them tight around his wrists. Then she led him into the street.

THE RADIANT ONE met with those on his list. The imminent attack could wait. The people had a reprieve. A moment to state once and for all on whose side they stood. They didn't realize the gift they'd been given. "God needs to know why you're here."

"All the others ran," a woman said quickly. "I didn't see anything else I could do."

"But the children," he said, motioning to the room full of them, some sleeping, some crying, and some listening. "Don't you think they will do what their parents do?"

The woman squirmed. "I've never been much for leading the way."

"All he asks is for you to be faithful. All you had to do was pray."

The woman leaned forward, head in her hands, weeping.

Left alone they were weak and helpless. "Next."

An older man, heavy around the middle, sat.

"I saw those red, hissing streaks in the sky. Thought it was the end of the world. What does God expect us to do against such monsters?"

The Radiant One was repulsed by the whining. He answered plainly, "He expects you to trust him with your soul and your life."

Every person was held to account. Some had stayed as long as they could, others had run at the first sign of trouble. Some were believers from way back; some wondered what God wanted of them.

Many weren't sure God existed.

How could these creatures ignore God's hand in the world? In their lives? The Radiant One would never understand the human mind.

60

"WHAT'S GOING ON?" Molly said. "Who are those men in white?"

It seemed the whole town was headed their way. Patch saw Jarrod's parents, carrying a spare set of crutches. Several teen girls gathered around Nancy, red-eyed. Even Granger showed up. Where had he been? Of course, he headed straight for Nancy.

Erin took Patch's hand. Molly and Claudia talked, laughed. It was like a big church picnic. Pastor Ron looked happy, though worry lined his forehead.

Encircling the crowd stood the men in white, looking like they had been riding cycles without helmets.

They towered over the people. Patch only hoped they were on their side.

Those who stayed praying were the only ones left. Maybe it was all over. He wished that they could be spared the final attack.

God have mercy, Patch prayed.

61

T REVOR WAS FRUSTRATED to be trapped in weak human form. It was attack time. What was holding them back?

Cowards. Fools. If he was there he'd be leading the way. Wiggling, he tried to reach the release on his costume. But he was too weak to snap the bonds. Once these humans figured out that his power came from their fear, it would be all over.

Why didn't somebody come to his rescue? His rage grew.

"Aren't you at least curious?" he asked, noticing McCry lick her lips.

"Sure. Show me how I can use that power. That's the only way you're going to get back to your kind."

"Yes, ma'am. I'll tell you whatever you want to know."

McCry hurried Trevor along. Why was she so anxious? He flexed his muscles and felt stronger.

That's it. She was afraid.

THE PRAYER CIRCLE was larger now. The sun was blocked by the demon hordes, glowing red.

"Please spare us, Father. Protect us." Pastor Ron led the prayers, and those who wanted to joined in. The majority stood watching. Around the perimeter the men in white stood shoulder to shoulder.

Then Patch saw her. Couldn't be. McCry, here? He had to be the only reason she'd come. Should he run? Be taken?

He decided on the direct approach. "Ms. McCry, Trevor, thanks for coming to the prayer rally."

There was no hope for Trevor, but McCry was another story. If Claudia could change, so could she.

"I'm taking you back," she said. Her smile made him queasy. Strange. Trevor was in handcuffs. These two worked together. What could cause her to bind him?

"Still offering that reward?" Claudia said.

Patch's jaw dropped like a stone in a pond. What in the world? McCry and Claudia had shared a lot in the past. They had worked together to imprison him. Now they were both here? Some coincidence. Had Claudia faked her change just to double-cross him? Had she summoned McCry? How could he have trusted her?

62

THEY WORKED IT out, Jarrod and his parents, apologies and for-
giveness all around. Jarrod confessed that he, too, had run.

"We should have set the example," his father said. "The prayer
rally was a chance to change this town, and we blew it."

His mother looked to the dark red skies, drooping like a weighted
parachute.

"It's like the picture in the museum," she said.

"But, Mom, this time we didn't all run."

"Will that make a difference?" she asked.

"Time will tell." Jarrod took her hand, squeezed it.

THE HORDES WHO'D fled were back. All of them. Everyone.

This was more like a picnic than a church service. Nancy liked
that. People brought food, and the tall men in white set up tables.

Lori and Miss Grady treated Nancy like she had a disease. And Granger had said hardly a word. What could he say? Where had he been?

"You say the men in white rounded you up and brought you here?" Nancy said.

Miss Grady glanced at Lori. Granger stood listening.

"Asked us all sorts of questions," she said. "Did we believe in God? Were we going to heaven? How could we be sure?" The woman lowered her voice. "I gave them the answers I think they wanted to hear."

Exactly the wrong thing to do; Nancy had learned that much. You couldn't fake faith.

"What about you, Lori?" Nancy said. Her heart had changed toward the girl.

Lori rolled her eyes. "I went along with the others, if it's any of your business. Those guys in white were pushovers. They didn't force us to give them answers."

Of course, they didn't. Nancy knew why. If they were on God's side, they wouldn't push anybody. Each person had to make the choice.

"God is real," Nancy said. "Don't you believe that?"

Snorting laughter from both of them.

Nancy told Ms. Grady she needed to talk to some of her other friends.

"If you're not back when the bus leaves, you'll find your own way back to camp."

McCRY DIDN'T LIKE the odds. She wasn't sure she could control

Trevor with this group around. And if Trevor got hurt, she'd never learn his secrets. She hacked off his plastic handcuffs with her pocket knife, and he pushed through the crowd between two men in white. McCry saw them grimace. But they did nothing to stop him.

She turned back to Patch. The reward was rightfully hers, but the home office would never give it to an employee. This was her job.

But with Claudia and Molly here, an idea struck McCry. She guided them far from the pesky praying, keeping one firm hand on Patch's neck. He wasn't getting away this time. Stumbling, he landed hard on his knees.

"So you get half and we split the other half?" Claudia said.

McCry liked this girl. She lowered her voice. "The paperwork will show that the whole reward goes to you."

"Because you can't collect the money yourself."

"If you want to be crude about it," she said, "yes."

McCry thought Patch looked pale. Good. Maybe he'd learn to pick his friends better.

Claudia patted Patch on his chest. "We just want to be clear."

"Yes," Molly said, making it obvious that she was turning off her phone video recorder. "I think Ms. Frazier will find this crystal clear."

McCry looked at them, then, without a word, she spun on her heel and left Patch, Molly, and Claudia standing there. But when she reached one of the tall guards dressed in white, he told her, "We can't allow anyone to leave once it's begun."

She just wanted out of there. "Once what's begun?"

THE RADIANT ONE gazed down on her. How to answer a skeptic's question? She wouldn't believe him no matter what he said.

"Demons from hell are about to rain down on you." He crossed his arms. "At least I think that's what's on the agenda."

"What?"

He watched the woman looking above. McCry finally saw the bulging eyes, flashing teeth, twisting tails, and it was obvious she finally understood what Trevor was about. She began to rage and curse.

"Ma'am, people are praying. You must be quiet."

She let loose another torrent, but when the angel said, "Hush," she fell mute.

YOU WERE TOO convincing," Patch said. "Like McCry, I bought every word of it until you showed the camera."

"After all we've been through," Claudia said, eyes twinkling, "still you doubt us? That makes me mad."

Patch couldn't blame her.

"You're annoyingly honest sometimes. You know that?" Patch gave her a hug.

"You too," Claudia said.

63

T REVOR WAS STUCK again. Back at the old fire pit with the tooth-less demons and those who'd proven themselves unworthy to join the attack. It was bad enough being shunned and spit at. This dank, crowded cloud was stifling. He could hardly breathe.

When he spotted his teacher looking down at the group pray-ing, Trevor flew toward him. Maybe his luck was improving. After all, he had escaped from McCry. Flabbygums would understand.

"Only one thing can help you," his teacher whispered. "Other-wise we're batting around a couple of other ideas: eat you or exile you."

"So what's the one thing?"

"Destroy Patch. Kill his friends."

Well, duh. That's what he'd been trying to do. McCry had proven worthless. He'd work alone from now on. No demon "helpers." Just him. Getting the job done.

This would be fun. Trevor planned to show his victims what horror really meant.

THE RADIANT ONE watched McCry. This woman's soul hung in the balance. If she did not recognize her need for God, she would die without him. So foolish, so pointless. The angel wanted to weep.

And she wasn't the only one. Many were mere spectators. They wanted a show.

And they were going to get one. At least, that's what the Radiant One expected. One could never tell about God, though. He was full of surprises.

Once the fireworks began, these people would have another chance. Stand or run. Let God guide or side with Satan.

Each would have to choose whom he would serve.

Not one would be left standing.

64

FLABBYGUMS, THE OLD devil, not only overlooked Trevor's escape, but he also said he was impressed enough to give him one last chance. Trevor's limbs swelled, his head stretched, and his human face hung behind him like a hood. He tore the costume to shreds.

If things went his way he would never wear it again, never have to wander the earth as a human. Trevor, the real deal, was back.

When the signal came, he would grab Patch first. Then he'd kick Jarrod's feet from under him and yank Molly's long, silky hair. Though he was alone, they'd think a swarm had struck. As for Claudia, the traitor, and Nancy, the one who'd shamed him, he had ideas so creative he could hardly bear to think about them. So many options, so little time.

Now that he was pumped and powerful again, Demon Girl and Guy sidled up to him. Maybe he could get some useful information out of them. "So why do you think we're not attacking yet?" Trevor asked.

Demon Girl said, "You don't know anything. Their prayers prevent us."

"So we're stuck until we get the decision to override?"

"That's pretty much it." She sharpened her claws against each other.

"I can stop their prayers," Trevor said.

"Sure, unless girls attack you. Then you swing them around on your tail." She acted as though she was covering a yawn. "We saw the video."

Trevor ignored them. He had to get down to the bluff, even if some said he wasn't allowed.

When the signal came, he'd scatter and squash those praying insects.

Until then he would plan his revenge.

First McCry had been provided a free flight courtesy of Trevor Airlines, and now her voice had been stolen. She had decades to go before retirement, but right then she would have traded her career to be a cashier.

McCry pried open her purse, found pen and paper, and scribbled:

Patrick: Get me out of here and I'll make sure you escape. From me. For good.

She signed her name. There. That made it official.

Where was that kid?

Patch FOUND IT nearly impossible to sit discussing the end of the world when a cosmic battle seemed about to erupt. What was taking so long?

Claudia looked to the skies. "Seems like it could happen any time." Patch nodded.

The subject changed as Jarrod announced his parents wanted Patch to live with them.

Patch didn't know what to say. What an offer. A home, family, a brother. He'd never thought a family would be possible for him again.

Suddenly Jarrod scrambled to his feet, grabbing his crutches. "Patch, run! Hurry!"

Too late. McCry had him by the shoulder. And he'd thought he was rid of her.

She shoved a note into his hand. He read it. *She* would help *him* escape? After all she'd been through, she still thought she was in charge. Despite the obvious clues around her, she was still trying to have things her way.

Patch stood to face her and could see immediately that she couldn't talk. She tried, expelling only air.

What an opportunity! Patch could give her both barrels, and she had to listen.

He told her how she, like he, was a sinner, that Jesus had come to earth to save sinners, and that she needed to receive him as her Savior.

No objections, no fussing. Patch could see by her face, though, that she wasn't buying it. She kept pointing at the note, gesturing, then finally tearing it up.

65

T HE MONSTER MIGHT have stopped her mouth, but he couldn't do anything about her mind. McCry returned to the tall man and tried to shove past him. She was determined to get out of there, but he proved to be as immoveable as granite.

McCry was forced to do something she hated—wait and watch. It didn't take long to recognize two distinct camps. Those on the outskirts paced, looking worried, stepping around the praying people. They clearly wanted out. She knew the feeling.

Others looked scared, but a few also looked smug. Most looked as though they had no idea what was happening.

Why would she want to be part of a group so clueless?

The big guy in shiny bright white—who was he and all the others dressed the same?

And that little creep, Patrick, couldn't see that she held all the cards. As soon as she got out of there, she would make sure he got what he deserved.

As for God, if there was such a being, he would never allow her to suffer like this. And if he did, she wouldn't have anything to do with him.

Our Master will give permission momentarily," the Shining One told the Radiant One. The Shining One swallowed, shocked, but he still trusted. God was going to lift his hand of protection from these people. He had heard their prayers.

"They won't understand," the Radiant One said.

"Not at first. They never do. Some might eventually."

"And us?"

"We are to fall back and break ranks. Let those who will run, run."

Soon they would find out where everyone stood.

66

VICTORY WAS CLOSE, Patch could feel it. He believed the men in white around the edge of the crowd would soon reveal themselves as angels. And save them. That was his hope.

Let the demons look over their shoulders. That wouldn't scare them. God was on their side. That's why he sent these men to watch.

As he and his friends softly sang *Amazing Grace*, he was reminded of all they had been through: ". . . many dangers, toils, and snares . . ." Including his own dread of being captured and turned in for a reward.

He'd never been safer than when he felt hell breathing down their necks. Worry was so foolish. All for nothing.

God had answered their prayers, brought them here safely. Expectation filled him.

JARROD WAS OVERWHELMED, overcome with the feeling that God was with them, in spite of his weakness, in spite of his fear, in spite of his failure. Was this the moment, the time, to ask once more?

Jarrod whispered. "Please heal me, God. Heal me now." A warm sensation shot through his body, and he knew God's touch, knew God was with him, in him. Should he throw down the crutches and leap to his feet?

Would that be the way to show his firm faith?

Words came to him, silently, and yet he heard every one. "No, my son. Not now, not yet."

God was with him, loved him. But the answer was still no.

Instead of anger or tears, joy bubbled from within. God was there and had heard him.

67

T REVOR HEARD THE gossip, wanted it to be true. Were they finally going to attack?

Flabbygums told some, "They're going to surrender."

What? Without a squeak, without a fight? That would be awesome. Trevor could taste victory. Let those pathetic praying people find out what it was like to deal with real power.

Someone suggested to Flabbygums that it might be a trap. The old teacher slapped the demon so hard his head snapped back. "Give our intelligence force more credit! Surely they would figure that out." Flabbygums jammed that familiar thick, clawed finger into the creature's face. "I should report you as a traitor."

If a break in the barrier was coming, Trevor wanted to be there, ready to join the attack.

But how would they know for sure the barrier was gone? Trevor wasn't going to be first, not again. He had made a fool of himself, thinking he could just soar down to the desert, only to find himself repelled by what felt like an invisible metallic roof.

Something was about to give. Row upon row of his fellow demons—those in the know—pointed their claws, spread their wings, opened their limbs. Now they fell toward the sparse enemy in an avalanche of red hot rage, like a volcano.

"You're mine, Patrick Johnson!" Trevor howled.

Sound denied had finally been loosed. The faster the demon horde descended, the louder they shrieked. Below Trevor the humans scattered or dropped. Most ran. Where did those cowards think they were going?

Trevor knew he would find Patch huddled on the ground with his friends.

Heads down, shoulders shaking, it was hard to pick one weak Christian from another.

McCRY WILLED HER feet to move, but she couldn't, not even an inch. The sky was a pitcher pouring out angry, flailing beasts.

The burly guards in white had backed away. *How could they leave us now?* One moment they were bossing her around, stealing her voice, and now they had retreated.

How dare they?

Patch's words pounded in her head. A sinner? Not her. She would never allow herself to think that way. She was a good person, always trying to do the right thing, doing her job the way she was supposed to.

Then why did she feel so rotten?

The flying things swooped, attacking, their disgusting stench filling the air.

McCry fought with everything in her to lift one foot off the ground. No good. Fear glued her to the spot. There was nothing she could do.

Nothing but pray.

Patch REALIZED HE had been wrong. When the men in white stepped back, he became convinced they weren't angels at all. They were the opposite. Traitors, demons disguised as the angelic host. The retreat made no sense otherwise.

Erin looked ready to run. "Don't!" Patch hollered, but she turned away and her legs flew. She reminded him of a solitary bird.

Granger didn't get as far. A demon slammed into him, crushing him to the ground, and Patch saw red streaks on his shirt.

"This isn't working!" Molly cried out. Patch could always count on her for a quick analysis of the obvious.

"So pray harder!" Claudia said.

Patch had the same choice everyone did: stay and pray, or give up and go.

He was tempted, but there was little hope in running from evil. The demons slashed and dove, snatching runners by their hair, lifting them into the air, and dropping them.

Patch could taste the terror, but his faith had not left him. He believed he was where God wanted him.

Then Trevor showed up. His eyes were huge, brows bulged. He looked puffed up, about to pop.

When he landed the ground shook, people ran past screaming. Pastor Ron dropped to his knees.

Trevor ripped Jarrod's crutches away, and when his friends and his parents tried to help, more winged beasts sent them sprawling.

"Pray with me!" Patch called out in a hoarse whisper. "Please!" Molly, Claudia, and Jarrod leaned in and formed a human tower of strength and protection.

But it wasn't working. Claudia screamed as Patch's hand was torn from hers. Trevor's claws dug into his neck as the demon separated him from his friends.

Molly was fighting to help Jarrod keep his balance. Whenever Patch fought to get back to his friends, Trevor met him like a linebacker. Eyes full of rage, he paused, hit, paused, hit, daring Patch to move an inch.

Patch's head throbbed, his neck oozed blood. Maybe he should run, distract Trevor from his friends, give them a chance to escape. No, that was his own deceitful heart, trying to justify saving himself.

Trevor swiped at Patch again, lifting him off his feet and hurling him to the dusty earth. The crash rattled his teeth. Now Trevor blocked his path.

Nothing was working. Patch was at a loss. God didn't always act the way Patch expected.

And as he struggled to return to his friends, his weary body gave out and Patch slipped to his knees.

68

"IT'S BRUTAL BUT necessary," the Shining One said, but that did not make it any easier for the Radiant One. He wanted to weep, watching the frightened flee.

So many wanted a Santa Claus-type God who showered them with gifts, who never said no, and who never allowed his children to be tested.

That was not who the Radiant One served. His was a God of power, who forgave freely but demanded loyalty.

As Patrick and his faithful friends fought, how the Radiant One longed to wade into the battle. But he would remain obedient, and for now his orders were to wait.

NANCY WANTED ONLY to protect Granger, but running never worked. She had to stand and fight. She could not allow Trevor to continue. She explained herself quickly.

"So you want to go back?" Granger said.

"No! I have to. I know that's what God wants."

She ran back toward Patch and the others, unsure whether Granger would follow. That was on him.

McCRY'S FEET WERE free. Finally, she found the strength to race away. She elbowed adults, shoved children, desperate to get to her car. The highway would be her escape from this nightmare.

As an officer of the law, she was sworn to protect the peace. But this was war. No one could expect her to stay and help. Only her own safety mattered.

But why the filthy feeling? The demons kept attacking, swooping like dragons, shoving and striking. She saw an elderly couple slammed to the ground, a small boy thrown on his side. Should she check on him, make sure he was okay?

No, there were too many. The rocky ground was covered with people crying for help. If there was a God, how could he allow such horror? This was his problem, not hers.

Truth was he didn't exist. It was as simple as that. So much for the idea of praying.

In her car, she turned the air conditioner on high but was irritated to find her soda was warm. It would have to do. All she wanted was to be away from this place.

In the distance, the red dust rose with the smoke, and flashes of light streamed across the sky. A one-sided affair.

More proof that God was a myth.

She'd have to write up a report. Thankfully, she was creative; she would think of a way to explain it to her boss. Sun spots. That was it. And an enormous dust devil obscured vision and made further observation impossible.

She sped through town, found a jazz station on the radio, and finally could start to relax. A sign on the outskirts read, "Visit Demon's Bluff Again."

Not if she could help it. Not in a million years.

69

CLAUDIA, MOLLY, AND Jarrod tried to help Patch, but it was no use. He was hardly holding up on all fours. Trevor seemed to gain size and strength by the second. Patch couldn't take another hit. For the first time he considered giving his life for this cause. This might be his time.

He could hardly breathe, his body weak from the beating. Trevor kept coming, shaking off the others with a sneer. Claudia's hands slipped off Trevor's tail. Their prayer seemed to avail nothing.

Where were God's angels? Patch sobbed in frustration.

Trevor looked him in the eye. He was his personal punching bag. His friends were distractions, only in the way. Trevor wanted him dead.

Every muscle and joint was in agony, but Patch refused to give up. Even if the angels failed him, God was there watching, hurting with him. He had to keep trying, keep praying. On his knees, Patch would face Trevor as he moved in for the kill.

His fear left him.

NANCY HEARD FOOTSTEPS, an attack from behind.

Not going to happen. No demon was going to bring her down without a fight. Patch needed her, that was clear. He was on his knees, wobbling, gasping. Trevor was hurtling toward him.

"No!" Nancy would be there in another breath.

Sprinting, she leaped and hurled into Patch, sending him rolling like a tumbleweed. Trevor smashed into her shoulder, and she heard a snap as she twisted. Trevor stood over her, foot pressing on her stomach.

She couldn't breathe.

70

WHAT COULD PATCH do but pray? He heaved in a gasp of air.

God help me. He felt blood trickle over his face, tasted the salty substance in his mouth.

His friends, who appeared to have been caught in some invisible net, struggled to sit up. And then he saw Granger.

It was David versus Goliath, but Granger had no sling. All he had was the unending supply of rocks afforded by the Nevada desert. He threw them as fast and furiously as he could, but Trevor remained with his weight on Nancy's chest, swatting them away like mosquitoes.

Erin knelt at Patch's side. "You're back," he managed. She helped him up.

The beast stepped off Nancy, faced Granger.

Trevor roared as Granger kept scooping rocks and firing.

Patch's throat was parched. "Please God, please."

In an instant, the pain drained from Patch and he felt strong. What was happening? He pulled away from Erin and went to help Granger. Trevor's jaws snapped open again, but not a peep came out. All over soaring demons banged into each other, cartwheeling to the ground.

THE SHINING ONE clenched a fist.

He and the Radiant One got the message at the same time: *help, save, protect all who have called on the name of the Lord.*

Suddenly the demons could no longer speak, roar, or scheme. God had allowed them to test his children, but not to take their lives. The beasts moaned and muttered as they fell. The angels unsheathed their swords and lightning lit the sky as they engaged in the ultimate battle for Demon's Bluff.

The Shining One and the Radiant One zeroed in on the demon who had targeted Patrick and his faithful friends. In seconds they cut him down, and he fell writhing and cursing God. He disappeared in a flash of white fury, sent to the fiery abyss where he would wait the judgment of all.

Trevor would never bedevil Patch and his friends again.

It was over.

71

NOT EVEN CLAUDIA could change his mind. His decision was final. Patch would strike out alone, let his friends catch their breath. He remained a fugitive, and it wasn't fair to expose everyone he knew to his heartache.

They all looked like escapees from a hospital ward. Bandaged cheeks and necks, arms in slings, torn clothes, but lots of smiles. Claudia wasn't used to that. She wasn't used to having real friends.

"You're sure you can't come back with us, Patch?"

He shook his head. "But thanks."

"Maybe we could take turns hiding you," Molly said.

Claudia wished she'd thought of it first. She looked at Patch, hopes high. He just smiled and shook his head.

"We have to figure out a way to stay in touch," Molly said. "A secret code."

Claudia liked that idea. She loved secrets.

ERIN FELT ONLY sadness. She cared about Patch, and what they'd been through brought them only closer. Why did good-byes always come? This was a hard one because it felt final.

Erin remembered running when she was needed most, and her shame burned. The others had forgiven her. So had Patch. Now she had to forgive herself.

"Tell your little brother I miss him," Patch said.

"I will. He loves you."

She wanted to say, "And so do I," but this wasn't the time or place.

JARROD HAD THAT look on his face and stayed back on the porch as Patch went down to wave to his friends. Only God knew if they would meet again. Patch wouldn't attempt to guess.

When he returned, Jarrod's disappointment was etched in his eyes. "C'mon, you know I want you to stay."

Patch embraced him. "Can't. McCry's people will be back for me. I don't want to get you in trouble. You know I'd love to. You're already like a brother to me. But I've prayed about it, and I have to move on."

THE TWO DEMONS were on their best behavior. Demon Guy would keep the name Barry. It worked for him. He wasn't as concerned anymore about getting in trouble. In fact, he was learning to like pushing the limits.

Demon Girl decided that Hope sounded sweet and harmless. Exactly what she wasn't. It made for a perfect cover. "Trevor's gone?" She still sounded doubtful.

"In the pit. Lifetime membership in the Sauna Extreme Club," the old mentor, Flabbygums, said. "I thought you two couldn't stand him."

"Yeah," Barry said. "I'm glad he's gone. He was bossy."

Hope snuffled. "He kind of grew on you."

"Don't get too attached to anyone," Flabbygums said. "The enemy is always trying to destroy us."

"I thought we were invincible." Hope's voice quivered. "That's what Trevor always said." Barry nodded his huge head in agreement.

The teacher scratched his scalp. "I'll let you in on a secret. Trevor lied. God can toss us into that bubbling broth whenever he wants."

"That's not fair." Barry stomped the ground, looked to Hope for encouragement.

"I'm not going to let him get away with it." Hope's eyes dripped gooey tears. Barry figured she was just practicing.

"Who?" Barry said.

"Patch. God." Hope straightened her pointy shoulders, clasped her claws together. "I'm coming after both of them."

FRAZIER STOOD OVER McCry's desk. "Not a word, ever." The woman's eyes darted, pleading.

McCry shrugged. "Then I need two extra weeks vacation and a raise."

"Whatever you want, as long as we come out clean in your report. As for the Johnson kid, he never existed."

"Who?"

Frazier smiled and tapped her high heels out of the office.

72

GRANGER SHIFTED IN his seat, touched the ring in his pocket. No one knew. His little secret.

He could use it when he got back. Get great grades, manipulate his parents, cream the competition during games.

What kind of reward might he get for turning in Molly and Claudia? Surely McCry would want to talk with them.

He had seen evil face to face. He'd fought for his Nancy. And that was all. He was her knight, no spiritual giant. He hadn't needed the help of those white-suited flyboys. All they did was stand around gawking.

He did what he did for his girl, not for God. Make no mistake about that.

Granger put his arm around Nancy and shut his eyes. Oh yeah, the ring would come in handy.

IT COULDN'T BE far to the next town, whatever it was. Maybe Patch could reconnect with the Tattooed Rats.

As he walked past the sign on his way out of Demon's Bluff, he smiled. The paint job was still fresh. With him leaving, the population stayed the same. The number on the sign said so.

But the name of the town was new. Demon's Bluff had disappeared from the map.

It had been reborn and christened Angel's Point.

Acknowledgments

I wish to extend heartfelt appreciation to the Men of Prayer who have uplifted me in my writing journey: thanks Aaron, Bill, Bob, Craig, Derek, Don, Ethan, Lynn, Mark, Patrick, Scott, Tom, and Wade. You are faithful friends. Thanks to my children—Jace, Jenna, Patch, Carol, Quentin, Cosette, and Tad—for their prayers through the years. And of course, deepest gratitude to Sue, the greatest prayer warrior I know.

—JP

About the Authors

JERRY B. JENKINS is the author of more than 150 books, including fifteen *New York Times* bestsellers. He is the author (with Tim LaHaye) of the multi-million selling *Left Behind* series. His *Left Behind, the Kids* series, coauthored with Chris Fabry, sold more than 10 million books. He and his wife have three grown sons and three grandchildren.

JOHN PERRODIN is a novelist, researcher, speaker, and attorney. He serves as Senior Editor for the Jerry B. Jenkins Christian Writers Guild. John and his wife Sue have been married for twenty-two years and have seven children.